# TARGET SIX

## (THE SPY GAME—BOOK 6)

## JACK MARS

# Jack Mars

Jack Mars is the USA Today bestselling author of the LUKE STONE thriller series, which includes seven books. He is also the author of the new FORGING OF LUKE STONE prequel series, comprising six books; of the AGENT ZERO spy thriller series, comprising twelve books; of the TROY STARK thriller series, comprising five books; and of the SPY GAME thriller series, comprising seven books.

Jack loves to hear from you, so please feel free to visit www.Jackmarsauthor.com to join the email list, receive a free book, receive free giveaways, connect on Facebook and Twitter, and stay in touch!

# BOOKS BY JACK MARS

## THE SPY GAME
TARGET ONE (Book #1)
TARGET TWO (Book #2)
TARGET THREE (Book #3)
TARGET FOUR (Book #4)
TARGET FIVE (Book #5)
TARGET SIX (Book #6)
TARGET SEVEN (Book #7)

## TROY STARK THRILLER SERIES
ROGUE FORCE (Book #1)
ROGUE COMMAND (Book #2)
ROGUE TARGET (Book #3)
ROGUE MISSION (Book #4)
ROGUE SHOT (Book #5)

## LUKE STONE THRILLER SERIES
ANY MEANS NECESSARY (Book #1)
OATH OF OFFICE (Book #2)
SITUATION ROOM (Book #3)
OPPOSE ANY FOE (Book #4)
PRESIDENT ELECT (Book #5)
OUR SACRED HONOR (Book #6)
HOUSE DIVIDED (Book #7)

## FORGING OF LUKE STONE PREQUEL SERIES
PRIMARY TARGET (Book #1)
PRIMARY COMMAND (Book #2)
PRIMARY THREAT (Book #3)
PRIMARY GLORY (Book #4)
PRIMARY VALOR (Book #5)
PRIMARY DUTY (Book #6)

## AN AGENT ZERO SPY THRILLER SERIES
AGENT ZERO (Book #1)
TARGET ZERO (Book #2)
HUNTING ZERO (Book #3)

TRAPPING ZERO (Book #4)
FILE ZERO (Book #5)
RECALL ZERO (Book #6)
ASSASSIN ZERO (Book #7)
DECOY ZERO (Book #8)
CHASING ZERO (Book #9)
VENGEANCE ZERO (Book #10)
ZERO ZERO (Book #11)
ABSOLUTE ZERO (Book #12)

# PROLOGUE

*Storage Basement Level 2, the Louvre, Paris*
*Midnight*

Maximin Béringer was getting very tired of sorting 18th century miniature portrait brooches. The Louvre, where he was a curator of Renaissance and Early Modern Jewelry, had hundreds of the things, and he had looked at every single one of them.

Sure, they were pretty—tiny little portraits often no larger than a postage stamp delicately painted by hand and enclosed in crystal before being mounted on a gold setting. They showed ladies with powdered wigs and impossibly large hats, or brave-looking officers in fancy uniforms, or smiling children who looked too pale to have ever gone out and kicked a football around like his two little boys.

They were delicate and expertly made, but more than a little dull after seeing a few hundred of them.

Béringer was assisting with a new exhibition called *France Before the Revolution: Courtly Style and Fashion of the Last Aristocratic Generation*, one that should be popular with the tourists. As for Béringer, he was a socialist and heartily glad that France's high and mighty had gotten the chop. Too bad they weren't doing an exhibition on the guillotine. That would have satisfied both him and the tourists.

Still, a job was a job, and if he wanted to take his wife and the boys on that vacation to Corsica next week, he needed to get his part of the exhibition sorted out.

Hence the long shift late into the night.

Béringer yawned. Time for another coffee.

Setting aside the tray of brooches, three orderly rows of long-dead faces looking up at him, he headed over to the espresso machine by the stairwell at the other end of the floor.

Béringer passed through silent rows of shelving, stacked high with protective boxes filled with everything from swords and gold tea sets to tricornered hats and landscape paintings. Béringer decided he really shouldn't complain. Despite his leftist leanings, he had always admired antiques and felt privileged to work in Europe's greatest institute of culture. A cup of espresso would improve his attitude.

Just as he got to the espresso machine next to the stairwell door, he heard the sound of several hurrying feet stomping down the stairs.

Béringer stopped and frowned. Other than the security guards, no one was here at this hour, and no one had business coming to the lower storage levels.

Even more surprising, they didn't stop at level two, where he was, but continued down to level three.

No one went down to level three. He had been working here fifteen years and had never been there. He didn't know anyone at his pay scale level who had been down there. It was said the museum's richest treasures were kept on level three, ones that were never shown to the public.

Of course, when a large organization has a secret like that, it spawns all sorts of theories. The resident medievalist said it was full of plundered art from World War Two that the museum didn't want to return. A janitor had solemnly told him they kept the pickled body of Catherine Monvoisin, France's famous 17$^{th}$ century fortune teller and poisoner, down there. Béringer didn't believe either of them, and leaned toward the opinion that level three simply contained some ugly but priceless artifacts, perhaps some rotted Egyptian mummies or bricks of gold hidden by King Louis XVI before the revolutionaries executed him in 1793. All very interesting, but not worthy of showing to the public.

Still, Béringer couldn't help but place a curious ear against the cool steel of the stairwell door.

It sounded like a  dozen people at least. A couple of them spoke in low tones, too quiet to make out the words, but he swore it sounded foreign.

Béringer suddenly felt nervous. What if it was a break-in?

The voices and footsteps faded into the distance. They had definitely descended to level three, a whole crowd of people going somewhere Béringer himself had never been. That was more than suspicious.

Even if there was a perfectly reasonable explanation, Béringer was justified in checking it out. The worst he would get would be a talking-to from whatever senior official was down there; the best he'd get would be a glimpse of what none of his colleagues had ever seen.

The third level below the Louvre.

Béringer shivered a little and tried to steel himself. He was not a brave man. While fit enough for his late thirties, he hadn't been in a fight since his schooldays. He told himself that if they were criminals, he'd sneak back to the ground floor and alert security.

And where was security, anyway?

He opened the door a crack and peeked out.

No one. Far below, he heard the buzz and click of an electronic lock opening.

Now thoroughly intrigued, Béringer tiptoed down the stairs, keeping to the wall so the people below couldn't see him in the stairwell.

Again he heard a couple of deep voices speaking in a foreign language.

After a moment he realized what it was—Arabic.

There were many Arabic speakers in Paris, so it was a familiar sound on the Metro and in the parks. Most came from Algeria, but this accent sounded different. What it was, he couldn't say.

The curator hesitated. He couldn't think of any on the security staff who would be accessing this level, and certainly not a whole crowd of them. The best thing to do would be to get back upstairs and inform the authorities.

But as he heard the group of people walking through that door, a door he himself had never looked beyond, his curiosity got the better of him. He had to see what was down there.

*And perhaps there's still an explanation,* he told himself. *Rich donors from the Persian Gulf? You wouldn't want to call the police on someone about to give millions to the institution.*

He knew in his heart that this was just an excuse, something to satisfy his urge to know; but it comforted him as he crept down the remaining stairs, ears perked to hear if the door closed.

*If they close it, I'll go right back up. If they leave it open …*

He didn't hear it close.

Béringer rounded the last turn of the stairs, and saw the doorway propped open with a storage box. Next to the door, an electronic combination lock shone with a green light.

He froze. Now he knew this was a break-in. No employee would use a box full of valuable artifacts to prop open a door and risk being fired.

*I really should go,* he thought …

… and ignored himself.

3

An overriding sense of curiosity drove him on.

He tiptoed to the edge of the door and peeked through.

Maximin Béringer didn't know what he had been expecting, but when he saw a large room full of shelves just like the one he had been working in, he felt a mixture of disappointment and curiosity.

Disappointment, because there were no gold bars or pickled poisoners.

Curiosity, because there must be hundreds, if not thousands, of artifacts stored on this level and none of them were listed in the general catalog.

What was the Louvre hiding down here, keeping from its own curators?

And where were the mysterious visitors?

More voices told him, in French this time.

"Please, you cannot take all these things. They're priceless."

That sounded like Alphonse Chaput, the chief curator.

"That's why we're taking them, idiot," a heavily accented voice replied.

"But you can't sell them," Chaput said. "They're one-of-a-kind objects. They'd be traced immediately."

A harsh laugh. "Do you think we're stupid? Only an idiot would fall for that."

Béringer had to agree. Every art thief, and every museum curator, knew that there were some wealthy collectors who didn't mind paying huge sums for precious artifacts they could never show anyone else.

Movement and conversation in Arabic. It sounded like the group was fanning out among the shelves and removing boxes, putting them one by one on the floor. The harsh voice from before gave what sounded like orders.

Despite the danger, Béringer had to see. He moved further away from the sound of the voices and crept along one of the aisles, trying to peek through gaps in the boxes to catch a glimpse of the intruders.

They seemed to concentrate on one side of the room, leaving him safe for the moment. Glancing at the labels at the ends of each aisle, he saw that the intruders were in the Ancient section, while he, at the opposite end of the large room, was in the Early Modern section. It was the standard organization for the other levels to run chronologically from one end of the room to the other as well.

He crouched for a minute, listening. After a moment, that harsh voice spoke in French again.

4

"Where is it, Monsieur Chaput?"

"We don't have it. It's only a legend!"

"My research says otherwise."

"Sure, lots of rumors say such a thing exists, going back all the way to the excavation, but it doesn't. I swear!"

Béringer crept to a closer aisle, trying to see what was happening by peeking through gaps between the boxes.

From what he could make out, they had all gathered at the far end of the room, a tight group of several men wearing black. He couldn't see the chief curator.

"Let me show you something, Monsieur Chaput."

Béringer snuck around the end of one of the aisles to get closer.

*Where's security?*

He thought he knew, and the answer made him shudder.

"My God!" Chaput shouted.

"That's right. We've been spying on them. We know where your wife works. We know where your daughter goes to school. If you don't cooperate, we'll kill you and then annihilate them on video in the most humiliating, painful manner we can devise. We are experts at this. Tell us where it is. Now."

Chaput started to sob.

There was a slap. "Cooperate. Now."

Béringer couldn't believe what he was seeing, but he snuck to an even closer aisle.

He could see better now. Squatting down, he peeked through the boxes and could see the legs of several men dressed in black slacks. Chaput stood between them, trembling like a leaf, a wet stain on the front of his pants.

"We mislabeled it to hide it. It's in a box labeled 'sword, 14th century.' Two aisles over."

Béringer looked around, his heart freezing. He was in the medieval aisle.

As quietly as he could, he hurried toward the door, praying the men who went to retrieve it would come around the other end.

He was in luck; he slipped around the corner just before the men appeared.

More talk in Arabic, then a gasp of surprise, even awe.

"You have done well, Monsieur Chaput," the harsh voice said. "We will not touch your women. They are no longer of any use to us."

"P-promise?"

5

"We have better things to do than kill a couple of infidel sluts."

"A-and me?"

"And you?" A laugh. "You get this."

A shot rang out in the storeroom, echoing off the concrete walls in a deafening roar.

Béringer ran. He ran out the door and up the steps, abandoning all attempts at stealth. Shouts and footsteps followed him. He ran up three flights of stairs and burst through the door, into the darkened ground floor of the Louvre. He ran as they pursued him. He ducked gunshots and jumped over the dead bodies of security guards. He ran until he outpaced his pursuers, and bolted out a side door and into the nighttime streets of Paris to find the nearest policeman.

# CHAPTER ONE

*A beach on the Greek island of Delos*
*The next day*

Jana Peters took another photo of the Temple of Poseidon, capturing the stone foundations of the wall and the few weathered marble columns that still stood. It was one of the many fascinating sites on what was, in ancient times, the holiest island for Greek civilization.

For the past few days, she and Jacob had been relaxing on this tiny island in the Cyclades, an archipelago in the brilliantly blue Aegean. It was three weeks since their last mission, and Jacob had shown a remarkable ability to heal. The bruises and cuts he had suffered at the hands of his torturers had all vanished, and his cracked ribs didn't pain him anymore. Only his shoulder, where he had suffered a gunshot wound, was still a bit stiff.

They had explored, hand in hand, all the archaeological sites on this lovely little island that had seen so many cultures—the Minoan fountain and the temple of Artemis, the rich palace mosaics, and the temple of Isis—enjoying a well-earned vacation at taxpayer expense. After what they had been through, they needed to get away, and an archaeological jewel that also happened to be remote with a permanent population of just 24 was the perfect choice. And all under an azure sky surrounded by sparkling sea.

Jacob had even managed to pretend more than a casual interest in all these wonders. Visiting the temple of Poseidon was a treat for him because it was right on the beach where he now lay, soaking up rays far out of sight of prying eyes that might be curious as to why his body bore so many scars.

Jana looked at him and smiled, but that smile hid a shadow. Her father, Aaron, who they had both long assumed to be dead, had saved them in Pakistan. From there they had escaped, first to the Gulf, and then here. The first few days in Athens had been chaotic, with Jacob in a military hospital recovering and all three of them having to go through extensive debriefing. There had been little time for a heart-to-heart talk.

Afterwards, her father had pulled her aside.

"I know you have a million questions, and I will eventually answer them all, but right now I have to go to Washington."

"Washington!" She felt like the bottom was falling out of her soul. She had just retrieved him from the dead, and now he was going on another trip?

"The top brass need me to fill them in on a few things, as I'm sure you can imagine. I am so sorry, but listen,"—at this point he held both her hands and looked straight into her eyes—"I will come back in a few days' time and we will talk about everything. Nothing will stop me from doing that, not even the CIA."

Despite all the past disappointments, despite all the broken promises, this time she believed him.

He had come back from the dead. That gave him a second chance in her eyes.

But she couldn't help feeling a tremor of worry, a note of doubt in the anticipation she felt for this day.

Because today was the day he was scheduled to come back.

Jana tried to lose herself in the ancient past, as she had so often done in her life. She wandered through the ruins of the temple, dedicated to the god of the sea, and ardently worshipped by ancient mariners who had to deal with the region's sudden storms and treacherous coastlines; she hoped some last remnant of that god's power would bring her father back to him. For he would come by sea. The island was too small for an airport and her father preferred to avoid flying commercially when he could help it.

"Too easy to track," he always said.

That, in a nutshell, was Aaron Peters.

Jana looked over at Jacob, who was peacefully snoring as the sun turned his skin the color of bronze. The last few days had been ones of quiet intimacy. Back in Pakistan, imprisoned by the Balochi regional authorities, they thought they were facing imminent death and had finally expressed what they had felt for a long time—that they loved one another.

Now, safe and sound, their natural reticence had taken over. Jana had always been an emotionally reserved person, no doubt due to her mother dying young and her father's long absences, and Jacob's job had made him put an emotional barrier between himself and the rest of the world. She also knew he was still mourning his former girlfriend, killed only a few months before in an assassination attempt aimed at him.

So they didn't speak about their feelings, instead sharing long walks, relaxed meals, and sitting close together by the campfires they'd built on the beach every evening. At the safehouse they slept in separate bedrooms.

While Jana enjoyed this new, relaxed closeness, she knew that sooner or later they'd have to talk.

But first, she needed to speak with her father.

A dot far out to sea caught her attention. It grew, resolving itself into a motorboat, its outline wavering in the heat.

She focused on it, slightly on edge. Ever since getting caught up in Jacob's life, she couldn't look at the most innocuous thing without wondering if it was a threat.

Neither could Jacob. At the sound of the approaching motor, he woke up and propped himself on his elbows to look out to sea.

Jana could see a single figure at the tiller. After a moment she recognized her father.

Jacob recognized him a moment later, and stood up to wave.

Her father waved back, and Jana felt a tug of jealousy. He had spent as much time with Jacob while she was growing up as he had with her, if not more.

And at least Jacob knew where he was back then. Jana had been left perpetually in the dark.

She shoved those negative feelings aside as she walked toward the shore. They were all lucky to be alive and back together again.

Aaron Peters cut the engine and the boat began to slow. He timed it perfectly, and the motorboat beached itself just above the waterline. Aaron hopped out.

Jana ran up to him and gave him a hug.

"You always like to make a dramatic entrance, don't you?"

"Hey, I don't want to disappoint. How are you two doing?"

"Relaxed and getting tanned. The ruins on this place are amazing."

"I thought you'd like it. That's why I chose it. I'm surprised you haven't been here before."

"I can't visit every ancient site."

"You could have fooled me. Hey, buddy. How's the shoulder?"

Jacob had just walked up. "A bit stiff but getting better. Still can't do any sailing."

"Soon enough, soon enough." Her dad got a distracted look.

9

"Everything go OK in D.C.?" Jana asked. She was almost afraid to hear the answer.

"Yeah. I had a mountain of things to tell them but that's all cleared up." He looked from one to the other. "And I have a mountain of things to tell the two of you. I've kept you waiting for too long so let's get to it. Why don't we go back to the safehouse and discuss it there?"

"All right," Jana said, her heart fluttering. Jacob only nodded.

They gathered their things and walked up the beach, inland over some rocks, to a stout traditional Greek peasant's hut, its whitewashed walls brilliant in the sun.

Her father turned to her, looking uncomfortable. "Let me speak with Jacob first and then we'll have a talk, all right?"

Jana swallowed the jealousy that rose like bile in her throat. "All right. I'll go sit in the garden."

There was a garden with a trellis of grapevines that provided shade, a peaceful place that she did not find peaceful as she waited.

She ended up waiting a long time. When Jacob finally emerged, he looked pale and shaken. He made his unsteady way past her, not even looking at her as he rounded the corner of the house and disappeared.

Her father, with the seriousness of a surgeon instructing a patient to get on the operating table, gestured for her to come inside.

# CHAPTER TWO

Jana sat in the little living room of the safehouse, facing her father. He was the same man she always remembered, rugged and fit, although she noticed new lines on his face and his stubble was speckled with gray. Both sat in wicker chairs covered in sheepskin. The whitewashed walls were plain but for an icon of Adrian of Nicomedia, the patron saint of soldiers. His somber face looked down on this father and daughter.

For a moment, neither spoke.

Then, with a visible effort, Aaron began.

"Missing so much of your childhood and young adulthood is the greatest regret of my life."

Jana didn't say anything. She had expected an apology. She'd had lots of apologies from him.

What she really wanted was an explanation.

"There's an old concept called the mathematics of power. Anyone in a position of power knows this whether they are familiar with the term or not. You have to make a tough decision. Either way, people get hurt. If one way leads to fewer people getting hurt, or more people getting saved, then that's the path you take. You do the numbers and make your choice.

"Like that Pakistani prison. The thugs running the place I don't care about. But the reinforcements, the regular recruits brought in to help guard you and the others, they were innocent. They were just young guys who thought they were fighting for their country, not knowing how corrupt their regime was. I didn't want to kill them, and when I could, I incapacitated them. I justified it because I was saving lives. Not just any lives, but the lives of operatives who I knew would end up saving more lives."

He beamed a smile. Despite the uncomfortable situation, despite her mixed feelings, that smile warmed Jana's heart.

"I've heard about the help you've given Jacob. Sounds like you've saved a whole lot of lives. That makes me proud."

"So you've been keeping track of us? Was it you who sent Jacob the warning when I was kidnapped in Mexico?"

11

"Yes."

"How did you know? Why didn't you come yourself?"

"I knew because I had been captured myself, and they had warned me not to resist because they had photos of you. So I waited until my captor checked in—he was supposed to check in regularly—and then I got out of my bonds and killed him. Then I made contact with Jacob, hoping he could free you before my captor's silence was noticed."

"So Jacob knew you were alive all this time?"

"No. I sent a coded message in a cipher only he and I knew. It half blew my cover, but it was worth it to save you."

Jana crossed her arms and frowned. "More mathematics of power? I'm just part of the equation?"

"No. You've always been so much more. It's killed me not to be able to spend a proper amount of time with you; it's just that ... " His eyes looked at the ground, and for the first time in her life Jana saw her father looking unsure of himself. " ... it's just that if I did, you would never be safe."

"You're saying I'm still a target?"

"Not specifically, at least not at the moment. They kidnapped you to get to me. They might try it again but I was speaking more generally. You're in danger, your friends are in danger, that shepherd you see in the hills in the morning is in danger. Everyone is in danger. All of civilization."

"From whom? The guys who kidnapped me in Mexico posed as neo-Nazis, but the local police didn't buy it. I don't buy it either. They didn't seem like radical Islamists either."

Aaron shook his head. "No, what I'm facing is a thousand times more dangerous. The Nazis and the Islamists are limited by their ideology. These people? All they really want is power and they'll do anything to get it."

"Who?"

His eyes briefly met hers, and then looked away.

"I can't talk about that."

"Is that who you've been fighting all this time?"

"I can't talk about that."

"Is that why you pretended to get killed? So they wouldn't come after you?"

Aaron shuddered. Another first. "No. I pretended to be killed so they wouldn't come after you. I had to lose you not to lose you."

"So who are these people? What do they want?"

"I can't talk about that."

"Jesus Christ, Dad! You're gone half of my childhood, then disappear from my life completely. You make me think you're dead, you make me and Jacob grieve, and you can't even tell me why?"

Aaron Peters kept staring at the ground.

"No," he whispered.

"I can't believe I'm hearing this."

He looked at her. "I am so sorry."

"Sorry isn't good enough! I deserve an explanation. Can't you see, Dad? I've been pulled into your world! I nearly got killed. I had to … to kill people myself."

"I trained you for that, but I hoped you'd never have to do it."

"Yeah, well I have, and it feels like a grease stain on my soul." Her father opened his mouth, but she cut him off. "And don't you dare tell me it was necessary. I know it was necessary. That doesn't make me feel any better about it."

"It doesn't make me feel any better about doing it myself."

Jana's frown deepened. "You chose this life. I didn't."

Aaron nodded sadly.

Suddenly Jana's anger was undercut by pity. This man had sacrificed so much, risked so much, in order to protect civilization. While that made him an absent father, he had done it for noble reasons.

But that wasn't the whole story. Aaron Peters was trapped, trapped by obligations and the burden of knowing too much. He couldn't look away. He couldn't stand idle. It would kill his sense of self-esteem, his honor.

He was trapped the way Jacob Snow was trapped.

He was trapped the way she, herself, was becoming trapped.

Because she had taken on those obligations, and she knew too much.

She had done more active fieldwork than some career CIA agents ever did. She had seen more danger, had more shots fired at her, and had stopped more terrorist attacks than most field agents ever dreamed of doing.

The sad thing, the really insidious thing, was that she found it thrilling. It was like a drug, and all three of them were junkies.

She put a hand on his.

"I understand. Well, sort of. You've done this far longer than I have and so I can't imagine it as a lifestyle, but I've been on five missions now, and I can hardly remember a time when I wasn't doing them. It's barely been a year, but my old life feels as remote as the Bronze Age."

Her father took her hand and squeezed it.

"Go back to it. Go back to the United States and take up your archaeological career again. It hasn't been disrupted too much, has it?"

Jana chuckled. "I've had so many sick leaves and personal days I'm surprised they haven't fired me. I have a feeling Jacob's boss has done something behind the scenes to help me keep my job."

"It wouldn't surprise me in the least. Tyler Wallace is a good man. I've been following your career as much as I can. That was an impressive mosaic you found."

For a moment, she didn't understand what he was talking about, then recalled that the previous year, just before she got caught up in all this, she and her crew had excavated a Roman villa in Morocco and had unveiled a gorgeously preserved mosaic.

It had been one of the best discoveries of her career, and she had almost forgotten about it after the storm she had been through.

She felt a longing for those easier, simpler days.

"I still have to finish writing that up."

"You're going to write a journal article?" her father asked, then chuckled. "I've read them all, although I have to admit I don't understand everything I've read."

"Yeah, they get pretty technical. But you have to publish your findings. I'm always criticizing archaeologists who excavate a place and never get around to publishing their results, or do it years after the fact when their memories aren't fresh anymore. Now I'm slipping into that bad habit."

"I think you have an excuse."

"True. Maybe things will settle down a bit and I can get back to research. Maybe we can all get back to something more normal."

She said that in a tone that invited him to become part of that, a half-uttered question as to whether he'd be coming back to the States too.

"Yeah," her father said, nodding while his eyes grew distant. "Maybe."

\*\*\*

Jacob sat shaking on a clifftop overlooking the Aegean. The scene was beautiful: puffy white clouds, blue skies, and crystal clear water.

He didn't see any of it.

All he saw was the horrible reality Aaron Peters had painted for him.

He had guessed some of it, that there was a higher war than the one he fought, that hidden powers on both sides had their own agendas, but he had never suspected the rot to run so deep, the threat so big.

And he never thought that he, Jacob Snow, the greatest anti-terrorist warrior in the world, would never have heard of the world's most dangerous terrorist organization.

The Order.

From what Aaron had learned, there could be nothing more inappropriately named.

Their short-term goals were to upset the balance of power in any way possible: set the Sunnis against the Shia in the Middle East, the Hindus against the Muslims in India, the Russians against the EU in Europe. Any weak point, any fault line, was ruthlessly exploited in order to widen the cracks of global society, with the ultimate aim of bringing it all crashing down.

And then? What The Order had planned after that wasn't entirely clear. Perhaps then was when the name would become appropriate. Perhaps then, from the ruins, they hoped to rebuild a new society along their own lines, with them in control.

What form this society would take remained unknown. The fact that they were willing to kill millions to get there, and even risk nuclear warfare, proved that whatever kind of society they would create would make Hitler's Germany or Stalin's Russia look like a pleasant democratic republic.

The worst of it all was that this group of crackpots was a vast and complex organization, with deep moles in systems of power around the globe, and with highly trained operatives who could match anything the established powers could throw at them.

This is what Aaron Peters had been fighting all this time. He hadn't come out and said it, but Jacob could tell this was why he had faked his own death, so that he could go deep undercover to combat this threat.

That cover had been blown somehow. The Order had kidnapped Jana in Mexico to force him to surrender while on a mission in Afghanistan. Those guys pretending to be neo-Nazis just outside Mexico City must have been Order operatives. Or at least those at the top were. When Jacob and his friends in the Mexican police and army

15

busted in there to free her, the kidnappers had wiped the computers and the last one standing had killed himself.

They would not be taken prisoner. Aaron Peters had been trying to capture one for years with no success.

Jacob looked longingly out at the sea, wishing he could live in a state of ignorance like so many. He wished he could hop on the sailboat he loved and just cruise around these beautiful islands, fishing and swimming until his hair turned gray. He wished the only fights he would see would be in novels and TV series, and that terrorists would only be something he read about in newspapers and, shaking his head, forget after a minute.

But he couldn't. He knew too much to ever live like a normal person. He couldn't close his eyes or turn his back. He had to fight.

Jana, the woman he cared about so deeply, couldn't close her eyes either. She was pulled from being a civilian into his dirty game and there was no going back for her.

And for that he was truly sorry.

# CHAPTER THREE

*Office of the President of France, Paris*
*The next afternoon*

Tyler Wallace had met three U.S. presidents, several foreign heads of state, and countless millionaires and other VIPs; yet he had never gotten used to red carpets, gilded columns, ceiling frescoes, and liveried servants. He was far more comfortable in an ops room checking out satellite data while talking to agents conducting a clandestine operation. When he was younger, he was more comfortable in camo with a Kevlar helmet and an M16.

He was also not entirely comfortable being the only black man in a palace. The last brother he'd seen had been a soldier at the checkpoint outside. The two had made eye contact as Tyler returned the sergeant's salute, and he and the sergeant had exchanged the tiniest of nods. That was the last friendly gesture he had seen that day or expected to see.

Still, duty was duty, and his duty right now was to talk with the French president and the head of the Direction générale de la Sécurité extérieure, France's equivalent to the CIA.

Why he, head of the Athens field office, was being called in instead of the CIA's man in Paris was just becoming clear.

The three men sat at a gilded table, an antique tea set sitting untouched in between them. The DGSE director, Monsieur Dubois, said,

"Thank you for coming here on such short notice, Mr. Wallace."

"I'm always willing to help my nation's allies. I served in operations with French Special Forces behind the lines in Iraq. Good men."

Monsieur Dubois nodded appreciation for this compliment.

"Then you are familiar in dealing with delicate situations. We have one now, and your superiors say you have the specialized personnel who can handle it."

"We'll help in any way we can."

The French president, a refined man with a noble face and wearing a suit that probably cost as much as Tyler's annual salary, took a drag from a slim cigarette, and spoke for the first time.

"This must be done with the utmost delicacy."

His English was a perfect imitation of a graduate of Eton, so perfect that Tyler got the impression that he added this upper-class accent deliberately, to show that he was not an Englishman.

"Nothing shared in this room will make it out of this room unless you explicitly say so," Wallace replied.

"You will tell everything to your operatives and nothing to anyone else. The Louvre was broken into last night by a group of Arab men. They took the chief curator, Alphonse Chaput, hostage, abducting him as he was going to his car after dining with some friends. Another employee spotted him being forced to divulge the location of a certain ancient Egyptian artifact in an off-limits storage area. They took this artifact, as well as several other priceless items. So far we have no word from them."

"Did this employee give a description of the men?"

Monsieur Dubois answered that. "He got a look at three of them, but only fleetingly as they chased them. Our best police artists made composite sketches. Here they are."

The secret service man handed over the sketches. Tyler looked through them. The sketches were all rather vague, the product of a panicked witness in poor light, running away. Tyler didn't recognize any of them, although they all had Egyptian features. The Egyptians stood out in the Arab world because they actually had very little Arab heritage. Genetically, they were mostly the same as their ancient forebears.

"Egyptians after ancient Egyptian artifacts? These men might have an interest in The Sword of the Righteous."

"So they may have been involved in the Suez Canal affair," Dubois said.

The year before, the terrorist group had stolen an ancient Egyptian Canopic jar containing ultra-rare, naturally occurring uranium-235. Uranium-235 is the isotope used in bombs and reactors. While it does occur naturally, it's generally locked in with uranium-238, a less radioactive isotope that can't sustain a nuclear chain reaction. Only twentieth century technology could extract the uranium-235.

18

But in very rare instances, U-235 is found on its own. The Egyptians had found some in their own country some time during the Old Kingdom, more than four thousand years ago.

The ancients had used it in magical rituals. The modern terrorists had used it to create a dirty bomb they hoped would block the world's busiest canal. The mastermind behind it all was a former Egyptologist who had been radicalized. At least that was the assumption. The man could have been self-taught, but they knew that whoever he was, he could read ancient Egyptian hieroglyphs. They'd been investigating Egyptologists ever since.

Those investigations had not revealed the archaeologist's identity or current location.

He didn't need to tell all this to the two Frenchmen. All this intel had been shared with every friendly power. It was too big to keep to one nation, and the French had been instrumental in rooting out cells of The Sword of the Righteous in the Sahel region of North Africa.

"Don't tell me there's another Canopic jar."

Dubois sighed, glanced at his president. Receiving a nod from him, he replied.

"Not a Canopic jar, but another example of fissile material from ancient Egypt. It looks like they're going to try a second time."

Tyler's jaw clenched. The Sword of the Righteous had come a heartbeat away from irradiating the Suez Canal and disrupting global trade for at least a decade. They had the expertise, the funding, and the will.

"So what is this thing?"

"It's called the Staff of Ra, discovered in 1932 by a French expedition in Egypt. At first the team thought it was a simple gold staff topped with the jeweled head of a falcon, symbolizing the sun god Ra. It was shipped to France along with various other objects from the excavation. Shortly thereafter, the head archaeologist and several of his assistants fell ill. At first it was thought they suffered from some rare tropical disease, but a physician finally realized it was radiation poisoning. The source was finally found to be the Staff of Ra."

"It's not shielded like the Canopic jar?" Tyler asked.

That ancient urn, one of a set usually meant to hold the internal organs of a mummified body, had been lined with lead to make it safe.

"It was. The staff was stored in a thick lead tube. The archaeologists had removed it from the tube. Fortunately they kept it, and once they realized the staff was radioactive it was put back in its

19

protective container, but not before four men died and several others fell seriously ill. When the authorities discovered the truth, they put it in a lead-lined box for extra protection and stored it in level three of the Louvre basement."

"I see. What else is stored on this level? Anything else that constitutes a potential threat?"

The French president looked uncomfortable for the first time. "Not a physical one, but the special storage level at the Louvre is used to house items that should not be seen by the public."

"Such as?"

He waved his cigarette. "Such information isn't necessary for the accomplishment of our current goals."

"You mentioned other items were stolen."

"Yes. We'll provide you with a list although these items are not of security concern. They are valuable, yes, and could provide some embarrassment to the French government, but they present no serious danger."

Dubois handed over the list as the president took a drag from his cigarette. Tyler ignored it for a moment.

"How much U-235 is in this staff? You need at least 50 kilos to make a bomb."

"There's only about ten kilos, so unless they have other sources elsewhere, and there's no evidence that they have, then they'll make a dirty bomb."

Tyler nodded. A dirty bomb was an ordinary explosive packed with radioactive material. When detonated, it would spread radioactive dust over a large area, making that area uninhabitable. The public thought the big risk from terrorists was that they'd make an actual nuke, but all nations conspired to keep fissile material out of the wrong hands. A dirty bomb was by far the bigger threat. All one needed was a big conventional detonation—easy enough for even a small terrorist group, and The Sword of the Righteous was one of the biggest—and enough radioactive material to fly out of it, which could take out several city blocks.

Set in downtown Paris, or London, or Berlin … and you have not only a high body count, but an economic ripple effect big enough to topple governments.

"Do you have any evidence as to where they went?" Tyler asked.

"Security cameras showed one man dressed as a security guard drive up in a delivery van to the parking garage. He had a forged pass that allowed him through. Once in, this lone individual went to a control panel and switched off the central alarm system. He also switched off the camera system and the phone system. It was a sophisticated hack. We have highly secure backups in place, and he circumvented them. We don't know how he got the plans but that doesn't matter at the moment.

"Of course, when the guard in the control room saw the cameras go blank, he went to check out what had happened. He must have teamed up with a couple of other guards because we found them all in a group, killed by knife wounds. The guard at the parking garage and a couple more in other parts of the building were killed in the same manner. The lone surviving witness said they shot the head curator, probably because no one would hear the shot down there, and also fired at him, probably because he was outrunning them.

"A security camera on the roof of a nearby bank caught the van leaving the area. We've pieced together a few other cameras from various buildings and discovered they got on a highway heading east out of the city. We lost them after that."

Tyler grimaced. "Considering how organized The Sword of the Righteous has proven itself to be, they probably had a private plane waiting and could be anywhere by now."

"We haven't tracked any suspicious aviation activity, but of course they could have flown below the radar with their transponder off."

"So we don't know where they are and we don't know what their target is," Tyler said gloomily.

"We'll get to work on this at the highest level. The field office here is entirely at your disposal."

"We do have a request," the president said.

"Anything."

There had been some friction between the United States and France over some foreign policy and trade issues, but none of that mattered in a situation like this. When the chips were down, the two nations were allies.

"We want the two operatives who foiled the Suez Canal attack to be on this mission."

"There was only one operative on that mission, a man named Jacob Snow, our best agent for the Middle East."

*Well, second best, but the best was under deep cover for so long even I didn't always know where he was.*

21

"We happen to know there were two operatives," Dubois said. "There was also an archaeologist named Jana Peters, the daughter of Aaron Peters. While she wasn't officially on the mission, her knowledge, and even her fighting ability, were vital in resolving the situation."

Tyler smiled. "Your agency has been doing its homework. The problem is that she isn't an official operative, as you say."

"Except she's managed to insert herself into several of your most important recent missions."

"She has indeed." Tyler wasn't surprised that the French had been spying on the U.S. Allies spied on each other all the time, to the extent that Tyler knew the name and bra size of Dubois's mistress.

"We want her on this mission," the president said. "Assuming she agrees, of course."

"I think she will," Tyler assured him. "She's hopped on every recent mission Jacob Snow has been assigned. They're very close so I don't see anything changing in this situation." Then he chuckled. "Except for the fact that we're actually asking her this time."

# CHAPTER FOUR

Jana woke early the next morning as she always did in this peaceful place. Here there was no Wi-Fi, no internet, not even a landline. Nothing to distract her from rising with the dawn, napping in the afternoon, and going to bed early after admiring the starry sky.

She got up and stretched, going through fifteen minutes of calisthenics in her clean but spartan room, with the window open to allow in the fresh sea breeze and warm Greek sunrise.

Now fully awake and hungry, Jana dressed and headed for the kitchen,

She stopped short before she even made it to the door of her bedroom.

A note had been slipped under her door.

Suddenly it felt like the bottom had fallen out of her world. With a trembling hand she picked it up and opened it.

It was in her father's handwriting, as she knew it would be.

And the contents were exactly what she had feared.

*My dear daughter,*

*I have said sorry too many times to you, and have no right to say it again, and yet I do not know what else to say.*

*I have to go. Duty calls. I must leave to keep the world, and you, safe.*

*I'll be in touch and will meet up with you soon, wherever you are.*

*Until then, don't judge me too harshly and remember that I am always ...*

*Your loving Dad*

*PS: Take care of Jacob. He's a good man.*

Jana crumpled up the note and threw it into the corner with a snarl. Running off again!

She stood there for a moment, teeth gritted, hands balled into fists, before she slumped, arms going slack at her sides. She walked over to the note, picked it up, and gently smoothed it out.

Then she sat on her bed and stared at it.

What if this was the last time she ever saw him? He was off on another mission, and she was left behind, wondering, like she had since she was little, if her father would ever come home.

Enough of this. If he had to go off to save the world, fine. That was his calling. She, on the other hand, wanted her old life back. She wanted to have some semblance of normality. Her job was waiting for her, along with a sizeable injection of cash into her savings account courtesy of the CIA. She could buy a house, get a little garden, work up the chain of academia and make full professor someday. The money was actually enough that she could even quit and just excavate and travel full-time for several years. She'd fantasized about that. While she loved teaching, the idea of complete freedom was a tempting one.

Whatever decision she made, she had to make it back in the States, back home, not stuck in a CIA safehouse, no matter how attractive that safehouse might be.

She started to pack, rehearsing in her mind what she'd say to Jacob.

\*\*\*

Jacob Snow may have been in a CIA safehouse on an idyllic island, but strange sounds still woke him with a start.

There was movement inside the house.

He glanced at the shutters of his window to see that it was still before dawn, not even a hint of blue to lighten the black of night.

Jacob got out of bed in an instant, grabbing his 9mm automatic from the bedside table and padding on bare, silent feet to the door.

There, he pressed his ear to the wood and listened.

He heard footfalls coming down the hallway.

Coming toward his room.

Slowly, Jacob backed up, leveling his gun, ready to fire through the wood if he had to.

The door was locked, of course. He always locked doors.

His night vision, sharpened through years of use, could just make out the rectangle of the door and the faintest light coming around the edges of the old, ill-fitting wood, as if someone had left a single light burning somewhere a couple of rooms away.

The light beneath the door was blocked in two spots.

Feet.

Then a darker shadow and the rustle of what sounded like paper. Jacob readied himself . . .

… and saw what he least expected to see.

A note passed under his door.

The footsteps receded and then he heard them stop by Jana's room. Again there came the rustle of paper.

Now he knew, without looking, what had just happened.

Aaron was leaving, and he was saying goodbye the only way he could bear.

Sadness and disappointment threatened to overwhelm him. He was glad no one was around to see his eyes filling up.

Jacob turned on a little penlight he had by his bed, shielding it with his hand and turning it away from the door so the thin sliver of illumination passing through his fingers couldn't be seen from the hallway. Most men wouldn't see it at all, but Aaron Peters wasn't most men.

*Dear Jacob,*

*I'm sorry I couldn't stay longer. There's nothing I'd like more than to spend a whole lifetime with the two of you on this island. But duty calls. You understand.*

*Please try to make Jana understand too.*

*And protect her. I know I don't need to ask, since you've done so much already, but things are going to get a lot more dangerous soon and you need to be on your guard.*

*I hope to see you soon.*

*Aaron*

Jacob turned off the penlight with a grimace. So he was off again, lost just after they'd found him. Gone off to hunt The Order.

Jacob fought the urge to run after him, trying to reason with him. He knew it wouldn't work. So he lay back in bed until he heard the distant hum of the motorboat carrying across the pre-dawn air. It dwindled away to silence.

Jacob grimaced and buried his face in his pillow.

He lay there, trying and failing to sleep, as the sky lightened outside and shafts of sunlight poked through the slats of the shutters.

Then he heard another sound, the sound of Jana cursing and moving around her room.

*Guess she found her note too.*

He felt torn between getting up and speaking with her and letting her cool off. Hell of a temper, that woman, and he didn't like being the target of it.

25

The movement down the hall continued. That got him curious, so he dressed, composed himself, and went out.

Her bedroom door was open. Inside, she was furiously packing.

"Um, good morning," he said.

"He left. Again," she said without looking up from her work.

"I got a note too," he said, leaning heavily against the doorframe. "I was hoping he'd stay this time."

Jana shot him a sympathetic look. "I can't do this anymore. I'm going home."

"Home? Where?"

"The United States. What do you think?"

"Oh. I haven't been there in a while."

"Want to come?"

Jacob blinked. "What?"

Jana shouldered her bag. "Come with me. My place next to the university is big enough for two, or you can get your own place if that's going too fast."

"Going too fast?"

"Just come. Get out of it. Quit your job and live like a normal person. Stop getting shot." She gave him a long look. "I'd like that."

"What would I do?"

Jana shrugged. "Anything you want. Be a cop. Drug dealers and car thieves wouldn't stand a chance against you. Or do security for VIPs. Personal security guards get paid well."

"You want me to be a security guard?"

"A security guard. A florist. A freakin' ballerina. I don't care! I just want you to get out of all this and come to the U.S. with me. But you have to decide now, because the one motor launch to the mainland leaves in half an hour. There isn't another one until tomorrow and I'm not waiting until tomorrow. I'm going to the mainland, getting a bus to the airport, and getting on the first flight home. Come with me. I'll even throw in first-class."

She walked up to him. Jacob gazed into her eyes. If she wanted him to come to the States with her, then that meant she wanted …

A phone rang in his bedroom. There were no phones in the house, no Wi-Fi, and no cell phone signal, so it could only be one device.

His encrypted satellite phone.

And if it was ringing when he was supposedly on R-and-R, that could only mean one thing.

Jana knew it too, and rolled her eyes.

She pushed past him and into the hallway.

"Coming?" she asked.

The phone kept ringing. He pointed toward his room.

"Could you hold on a minute?"

"No."

The phone rang again.

"Pack and join me. Please."

Another ring. Tyler Wallace would be getting worried.

"I, um … hold on."

He ran into the room to answer the satellite phone, knowing that when he came back into the hallway, Jana would be gone.

***

Aaron Peters sat in the motorboat as the early morning breeze blew in his face and a newly risen sun turned the Aegean Sea golden. The sight should have made him feel serene and at peace.

He remembered that feeling, or at least he thought he did. It had been so long since he had felt anything close that the words had become mere abstractions, like "paradise" or "perfection." Something to long for but never attain.

Seeing Jana and Jacob again had been wonderful; even in the heat of battle when they were fighting for their lives and couldn't speak, he had felt a closeness and a belonging he hadn't felt in years.

It had been all too quick. Once they got out of danger, Orhan flying them from Karachi to the Gulf and then on to Greece, there had been days of debriefing, long days of consultation with the collected heads of the CIA, MI6, and half a dozen other nations' spy agencies to go over what he had learned, go over satellite data, review what each agency had discovered.

It had felt like a poker game because he knew for a fact that at least some, and perhaps all, of those agencies had been infiltrated.

Which is why even Tyler Wallace didn't know his next move.

All these long years fighting The Order had been nothing but skirmishes. He had probed, spied, and taken out small cells of the organization. He had tried half a dozen times to capture one of their operatives, but every time they had either gone down fighting or bitten one of those damn cyanide capsules and taken their own life.

In all this fighting, he had done no real damage to their organization. The Order brought in new recruits as quickly as he could eliminate them.

But he had gathered enough intelligence to go to Phase Two. Now he'd level up from skirmishing to a real battle. He'd found a weak point, and he was going to hit The Order where it would hurt.

While he knew it wouldn't be enough to take the whole stinking edifice down, it would put them on the back foot.

The real concern was what their reaction would be.

Whatever it was, it wouldn't be pretty.

But maybe that would be enough to wake up the world to the real dangers facing it.

And distract The Order enough to keep them from targeting Jacob and Jana.

Tyler Wallace had already told him they'd be in the safest place possible—the front lines, where they'd be constantly on the move and on the alert.

To protect the two people he loved the most, he had to put them in danger.

"I'm sorry," Aaron Peters whispered as his motorboat sped across the crystalline water toward the mainland, where Orhan would be waiting to fly him to the next battlefield.

"I'm sorry."

# CHAPTER FIVE

Jacob picked up the satellite phone and heard his boss's familiar voice on the other end.

"Agent Snow, how are you recovering?"

"The shoulder is nearly healed, sir, and the other injuries are gone. My ribs are still a bit tender."

"We have a situation."

"We always have a situation!" Jacob snapped, opening the shutters in the hopes of seeing Jana.

"I beg your pardon?"

"Nothing, sir."

That's what he was seeing, too. Nothing. Jana had gone down the other path to the jetty.

"Is everything all right?" Wallace asked.

*Nothing gets by this guy.*

"Everything is fine, sir. It's just odd having Aaron back."

"And losing him so soon. I'm sorry, Agent Snow."

"It would have been nice if you could have told me."

"You know I couldn't."

"I know, I know. Sorry. So what's the situation?"

"We think The Sword of the Righteous is back on the scene. A group of Egyptians broke into a secret vault in the Louvre and stole some items."

"I'm thinking Greek statues and Louis XIV furniture don't constitute a threat to international security?"

"No they do not. The thieves stole a number of items, all of which could be embarrassing to the French government, but only one is of real danger—the Staff of Ra."

"The ancient Egyptian sun god?"

"Jana Peters is rubbing off on you."

"She is."

*And she just ditched me too.*

"How is she?"

He glanced toward the open window. "A bit emotional because of the situation with her dad."

29

*And with me.*

Jacob still hadn't decided what he thought about all of that.

"I can't even imagine. Is she fit for duty?"

"What?"

"She was injured in the last mission. Is she fit for duty?"

"Just some bumps and scrapes, plus a graze from a bullet. Yeah, she's fine. You're not suggesting she's … "

*Of course that's what he's suggesting, idiot, otherwise he wouldn't ask.*

"Let me fill you in on the details. The French government has just been given a warning that if they don't hand over a billion euros within twenty-four hours, there will be reprisals. Oddly, they haven't said what. Even just revealing what they stole would be reprisal enough, but that's not how terrorists roll. It will be something violent."

The euro was worth slightly more than the U.S. dollar, so that was more than a billion dollars. Easy enough for the French government to pay, but far more than any other demand ever made by a terror group.

"Have they said they're Sword of the Righteous?"

"No. That's only an assumption based on the fact that they're Egyptians going after fissile material in an ancient artifact. The Staff of Ra contains ten kilos of naturally occurring U-235."

Then it was a good assumption, although not an ironclad one. In the secretive world of terrorism, with its constant deaths and shifting alliances, specialists like bombmakers and other experts often moved from one group to another. The professor who must be behind all this could have gotten a job with a new outfit.

Tyler Wallace went on.

"The thieves seem to have gotten out of the country without being traced, but French intelligence has picked up a recent spike in chatter from a group called Eternal Jihad."

"Who?"

It was rare for Jacob Snow not to have heard of a terrorist group.

"They're a splinter group who broke away from Al Qaeda in the Islamic Maghreb and pledged allegiance to The Sword of the Righteous after the Suez Canal attack."

Jacob grunted. "Even a failed attack brings in recruits if it's that big of a score."

"All too true, my friend. And it wasn't an entire failure. They blocked the canal for several days. Estimates are more than two billion in lost global trade revenue."

"If people knew what those crazies were actually planning, every stock market on the planet would have crashed."

"Exactly. Anyway, Eternal Jihad have a base deep in the desert of Chad. There's been a spike in chatter, and most importantly a message that a delivery had come from France yesterday. We're getting intel from the French government and a group of French Foreign Legionnaires are being scrambled to make the raid. An airstrike would be too clumsy. We need to make a precise hit, take out the threat, and retrieve the objects. You and Jana will fly to Aswan, where you'll liaise with the French in the western desert of Egypt and head out on the mission. The Egyptians are giving their permission and the French will provide the arms and air support."

"Why do they want Jana?" he asked, unconsciously glancing at the door even though she wouldn't be there.

"Her contributions on your last few missions has become known to many intelligence agencies. They want her along for her archaeological expertise, her knowledge of Arabic, and her ability to stay cool in extreme situations."

"But she's a civilian!"

*And an angry one at that.*

"She's hardly a civilian, Agent Snow."

"She left this morning. She's on her way back to the States."

"Oh. That's bad. Follow her and ask her. Try to convince her how important this is. It's her choice whether she comes or not, but seeing as she's Aaron Peters's daughter, I think she'll say yes."

*I'm not sure I share your enthusiasm. Plus I have to catch her first.*

*And I'm not sure I want to convince her. She's been put through way too much already.*

***

Jana stood at her gate at Athens International Airport, arguing with the woman at the ticket counter about the size of her duffel bag.

"I am sorry, madam," the woman said in heavily accented English. "Your bag has to fit in this space."

She pointed to an impossibly small box next to the counter, her extended finger tipped with a perfect nail, freshly painted a deep red.

Jana kept her nails short so she could do the manual labor of excavating archaeological sites, and even so they were chipped and cracked. She never bothered to paint them.

"I can fit it in there," she said, stuffing the bag in with an effort. "It's all just clothes and a couple of other things. No sweat."

"You cannot crush it. It must fit naturally."

"Don't be ridiculous! You said fit, and it fits!"

"Could you hurry up, please?" moaned a middle-aged man and his wife behind Jana. They were American, soft around the middle and sunburnt in the face and arms.

Jana ignored them. "Look, it's in there. That's good enough."

Before the airline employee could reply, the tourist guy cut in again.

"We paid a lot for this vacation."

"Nobody cares," Jana snapped. She turned back to the employee. "I'm in a hurry, and I don't want to wait for my luggage in JFK. This fits fine."

"I can't believe this," the tourist guy's wife said, tossing her bottle blonde hair. She pulled out her phone and started narrating. "We're here in Athens airport, and this person—"

Jana whirled around, putting a hand over the woman's phone camera, and glaring at the couple with such intensity they froze in place like a pair of classical statues, if classical statues were more realistic about depicting the human form in First World decay.

"Do. Not. Film. Me."

"Madam," the airline employee said. "Perhaps we should all calm down."

Just then, Jana received a very good reason not to calm down.

Jacob showed up, with a Greek police officer next to him. The cop had probably been Jacob's ticket into the departure area.

What was he doing here? Was he coming along? She didn't see any baggage.

Before she could react, the tourist woman stepped forward and addressed the policeman.

"Officer, I am so glad you're here. Do you speak English?"

"Yes."

"Great!" She pointed an accusing finger at Jana. "This woman here was being really rude and not following airline instructions. When we pointed out her bag was too big, she nearly attacked us! I want her arrested. I have evidence. I filmed the whole thing."

She held up her phone triumphantly.

"May I see that?" the policeman asked.

"Sure. The video's right here. Just watch how she behaves."

Without skipping a beat, the police officer took the phone and deleted the video.

"What the heck are you doing?" the tourist screeched.

Her husband stepped forward, swaggering in a bad imitation of an action hero.

"Listen, buddy. That's my wife's private property. You had no right to do that. I'm going to take your badge number and call the embassy. I'll have you fired."

The officer looked at him coldly. "You are interfering with police business. Step to the back of the line or I will have you detained."

The couple sputtered, but did as they were told. Jacob and Jana stepped away from the crowd. The police officer kept his distance.

"What are you doing here?" she asked.

"There's a situation."

"So?"

"You've been asked to help."

That stopped her. "Huh?"

She was accustomed to making more intelligent replies, but it was the only thing she was capable of uttering at the moment.

Jacob looked unsure of himself. "You, um, don't have to if you don't want to."

Jana glared at him. "I'm aware of that."

"Um, OK. Well, I had to ask." He made as if to turn away but didn't actually leave. God, this guy was annoying.

Jana sighed. "So what is it?"

"More naturally occurring U-235, this time in some artifact called the Staff of Ra."

"The Staff of Ra doesn't exist. It's an archaeological conspiracy theory."

"Yeah, well your conspiracy theory just got stolen from the Louvre."

Jana blinked. "By whom?"

"It might have been our old friend the rogue Egyptologist, plus a gang of his gun-toting buddies. It's been all over the news except we were isolated on Delos and didn't hear about it."

"My God."

"They failed last time, so they're trying again. And Wallace wants you on board."

"Why?"

"You know why. The French government wants you on board too. Asked for you by name."

She crossed her arms. "Jacob, I told you just a couple of hours ago I want to go home."

"Come on, I chased you all the way here. I had to bribe a fisherman to take me to the mainland, then called in a favor with the Greek police."

"The Greek police owe you favors? I figured it would be the other way around."

"Well, actually it was someone else's favor, but that means I owe her a favor."

"Her?"

"Operative. Old and married. No threat to you."

Jana's frown deepened. "You're getting awfully presumptive."

Jacob gave that annoying, boyish grin he thought always won over every woman's heart.

"Hey, you invited me to live with you in the U.S., remember?"

"And you ran off to talk with Wallace."

"Duty called. Literally. Come on, Jana. We need you. I promise to keep you out of danger if you'll actually help me keep my promise this time."

Jana rolled her eyes. "You're unbelievable. I'm getting on this flight."

"Why? So you can argue with someone behind the counter about the size of your carry-on? So you can get lectured by sunburned tourists? And when you get home, what then? The morning commute? Trips to the supermarket? Catching your students cheating on tests?"

Jana glanced at the line that was slowly filing forward, each person getting their boarding pass scanned. *Beep beep beep.* They passed through the reader like little electronic sheep.

"You're not made for that, Jana."

With those six words, Jacob deflated all her half-formed plans.

No, she wasn't made for that, and even if this annoying man she cared about so much hadn't said anything, the thrill of another hunt for an ancient artifact, the sense of duty in stopping a global catastrophe, and the pride and obligation that engendered meant she could never board that plane.

It was a pity. She wanted to pour her complimentary glass of Greek red wine over that woman's head.

Jana let out a deep sigh.

"All right. What's the plan?"

# CHAPTER SIX

*The desert of central Chad*
*The next evening ...*

The chopper thudded low and fast over the desert. Out the open door, past the door gunner with his heavy machine gun, the sand dunes sped below, looking in the moonlight like an undulating silver sea.

Jacob looked back at the team, a score of heavily armed men of the French Foreign Legion, all grim-faced and poised for action. Each man, and Jacob himself, wore a Kevlar helmet and vest. Each was armed with a FAMAS F1 assault rifle, a well-designed, compact weapon that, while not Jacob's first choice for a primary arm, was still a damn good firearm. Each man also had a PA MAC 50 9mm sidearm and four grenades, two each of fragmentary and flash bang. A couple of the huskier guys carried AA 52 machine guns with bipods.

Another guy carried a LRAC F1 rocket launcher in case the intel was wrong and they came up against armor. It would also come in handy for busting down the gate of the old French colonial fort the terrorists were holed up in in case they didn't have time to set the C4 Jacob carried in a satchel.

No one carried sniper's rifles. No need. They were going in fast and close.

Jacob turned to Jana, who looked out of place although she had an assault rifle, sidearm, and Kevlar as well. She was supposed to stay with the chopper and only come in if they needed consultation.

"Doing good?" he shouted over the thudding of the chopper blades.

Jana nodded, tense, on edge, but ready. He'd never seen a civilian so ready.

Only a half-civilian, as Wallace had pointed out. She was Aaron Peters's daughter.

"Antoine will take good care of her," shouted the guy with the rocket launcher.

Antoine was the pilot and would stay with the chopper too.

"They won't have to wait long," Jacob said. The plan was to land five miles away, far enough that the terrorists wouldn't hear the chopper, and quick march to the fort. Then they'd unleash hell on the bad guys and come on back with the loot.

That was the plan, anyway. Raids never went according to plan.

The guy with the rocket launcher raised a fist. "I've fought these idiots before. We'll crush them."

"Too bad we're not going after Germans."

The guy gave him a cold stare. Jacob grinned at Jana and jabbed a thumb in his direction.

"French people. No sense of humor."

Jana rolled her eyes. She didn't have much of a sense of humor either. She'd been grumbling and uncommunicative for the past day, ever since agreeing to go on the mission.

Why? She usually followed him until they were in deep enough trouble that he had no choice but to let her come along.

Ah well, she'll be better once they started to save the world. That always seemed to cheer her up.

An announcement crackled over their headsets in French. Jana opened her mouth, probably to translate, then got cut off when the pilot Antione repeated himself in English.

"Touchdown in one minute."

Everyone checked their weapons and gear, including Jana.

Jacob glanced out the window again. The desert floor was coming up fast. He didn't see any movement out there. More importantly, the door gunner, with IR goggles, didn't see any either.

If Eternal Jihad really did bring the goods here, they obviously thought no one knew they had taken over the old fort. This whole region was dotted with terrorist bases. He'd taken out a couple himself.

As they came closer to ground, he could see the dunes had given way to flatter terrain with scrub, grasses, and the occasional spindly tree. They had passed through the desert proper to what was known as the Sahel, a long strip of land that was still basically desert but not the desiccated wasteland of the Sahara. There was ground water if you dug deep enough in the right spots and weren't too picky about the flavor of what you drank, and just enough plant life to support small herds of sheep and goats.

There would be people here. Nomads, mostly, with a few scattered villages at the oases. The grasslands and jungle of what people usually thought of as Africa was still hundreds of miles to the south.

They touched down. The squad leader, a captain named Vincent, let out a shout while everyone cheered and piled out. Jacob was last in line and as he leapt through the doorway, Jana grabbed him by the arm.

"Come back," was all she said.

*\*\*\**

The fort gleamed in the faint light of the moon, which was just setting in the low dunes to the west. From where he lay behind some scrub, Jacob saw a stout stone fort a hundred feet on each side, with towers at each corner. Those towers and the tops of the walls had crumbled somewhat from age, and Jacob wondered how strong those walls really were.

Good enough to stop small arms fire, at least.

That big wooden gate wouldn't stand a blast from a shoulder-mounted rocket, though.

But before they went in like a scorching desert wind, they needed to get closer. With a whispered command, the team put on their IR goggles and the scene shifted to a weird dreamscape of grainy greens and black. Jacob picked out two—no, three—figures in the towers, brighter points of green against the background.

"Intel says this group doesn't have any IR capability," Captain Vincent said next to him.

When ISIS overran the Iraqi armed forces a few years before, they captured a huge supply of American-provided equipment, including hundreds of IR goggles. Some of those had made it onto the international arms market.

"Let's see if your intel is correct," Jacob said.

"Stick close to me or Pierre," the captain said, indicating the man on Jacob's right. "We speak the best English, although we all can speak it well enough."

"We'll be speaking a universal language before long," Pierre said with a grin.

The captain gave a command and the men got up and started jogging forward, bending low to make less of a profile. While the gate was only two hundred yards away and well within range of the rocket launcher, and hitting it would be literally like hitting the broad side of a barn; they needed to get in close, because once that rocket went off, they'd lose all advantage of surprise.

They'd only gone about a quarter of the way when a cry from the fort showed they'd already lost it.

A shot cracked the night air. Jacob saw a brief flare from one of the towers.

"Your intel was wrong!" Jacob shouted as he and the others went prone.

With a loud click, floodlights shone atop both towers and two more on the wall in between. The lights flared painfully in Jacob's eyes and he tore off his goggles.

"OK, not entirely."

If they had to switch on floodlights, then only the sentinels actually had IR goggles.

Captain Vincent gave an order and everyone opened up. Blinking through the purple afterimages in his eyes, Jacob joined in too.

For the first few seconds their fire was inaccurate, but as the men's eyes adjusted to the light, first one, then two of the floodlights got taken out. That dimmed the glare enough that they could see better.

Another barked a command. The guy with the rocket launcher got on one knee and fired.

The rocket streaked through the intervening space to hit the gate right at the spot where the two doors met. The doors blasted apart, one swinging wide open, the other splintering, the remains hanging on its hinges.

But that flimsy old historical relic was only the first line of defense. Right behind stood a pair of technical vehicles, jeeps with heavy machine guns mounted on them.

Both of those machine guns opened up.

Everyone hit the dirt as the heavy rounds tore up the sand all around them. A man cried out to Jacob's left. Jacob risked his life to rise a little and return fire. His bravery got rewarded by seeing the terrorist manning the righthand machine gun flail and fall.

The other one kept firing, pinning down the French unit.

The man with the rocket launcher rose again to fire, then flew back as bullets hammered into his Kevlar.

Jacob crawled over to him. The man lay moaning, eyes hooded in shock. Jacob grabbed the rocket launcher, a LRAC F1 that he had seen a tutorial video for but never held, looked it over in the dim light, and decided he could fire it.

Someone shouted something to him in French, too excited to remember to speak English. Jacob decided to ignore him. If the guy

39

didn't have the courtesy to address him in a language other than the one used by his own unit, he didn't deserve a response.

Jacob rolled to his left, past a couple of other legionnaires, and raised himself up.

He fired. To his delight and mild surprise, he got it right the first time.

The rocket hit the lefthand jeep right in the body. The entire vehicle flipped backwards, its gas tank lighting in midair and bursting with a fireball that enveloped the jeep next to it.

Captain Vincent shouted an order over the din. Everyone rose and charged except for the man at each end of the flanks, who laid down cover fire. Jacob dropped the rocket launcher, readied his assault rifle, and charged too.

For a moment the defenders were too stunned to respond. The gas tank from the second jeep lighting up and bursting in a deafening roar kept them off balance for another precious few seconds.

And then small arms fire opened up all along the fortress wall.

# CHAPTER SEVEN

Jacob ducked and zigzagged as bullets flew all around them. The defenders, still shaken and half blinded by the inferno at their gate, fired wildly, some on full auto. Still, that was enough to fill the air with lead, and it was only a matter of time before more of the guys would go down.

They had to get to the gate and they had to get there now.

The question was—would the flames be too much for them to actually enter?

First things first: they had to get out of this killing zone.

The two legionnaires on their flank fired grenade launchers at the fort, but at such a long range their fire was inaccurate. The first grenade bounced off the top of the tower to detonate at its base. The second sailed right over the wall and exploded somewhere inside.

Still, that and the running fire from the advancing French line was enough to rattle them. Some of the defenders ducked for cover. Others kept firing, and another legionnaire went down.

A hundred yards. Eighty. The fire lessened, but Jacob knew the jihadists inside were preparing to meet the assault. The flames at the gate still burned high and hot. If they couldn't get in, they'd be pinned to the base of the wall and all the defenders would have to do would be to drop grenades down on them.

The guys on the flanks took care of that. The next two grenades zeroed in on their line of advance and detonated right inside the gate. One knocked a jeep back several feet. The other blew up right in the middle of the inferno.

The two grenades acted like a pair of giant feet stomping on the fire, blowing much of it out by spreading the flaming gas in an even wider radius, thinning it so that it quickly burned itself out.

Jacob hoped it had set fire to some jihadists hiding nearby. More importantly, it cleared the entrance of most of the flames.

Letting out a final burst along the top of the wall, Jacob ejected his magazine and slapped in a new one. The worst thing in a close-up firefight like this was to get caught short.

41

The men on the flanks lobbed a couple more grenades over the wall, another Frenchman fell, and then they were almost at the gate.

Jacob came in, dead center, pelting across the steaming sand, the searing air heavy with the stench of burnt gasoline and flesh. Two legionnaires took the flanks, throwing grenades around the corners before daring to show themselves. The moment after those blew up, Jacob passed through the gate. Through the flames spouting up out of one of the upturned vehicles he saw crouched figures beyond. He fired and one went down, then he jerked to the left and return fire screamed back at him.

He leapt over a puddle of flaming gasoline, landed on the far side, and took out another jihadist who was just coming down the stairs on the back side of the wall by the gate. He sprayed some vague forms to his right and ran up the steps. Too much smoke and fire on the ground level, and with afterimages still dancing before his eyes, he could barely see a thing. He hoped the jihadists couldn't see much either.

At least one could because a bullet cracked off the stone wall just ahead of him. A moment later, another shot took out a chunk of the old crumbling step at his feet. Jacob kept going. The tempo of fire rose as more of the Frenchmen charged into the fort.

No more shots came his way. The guy who had a bead on him was either dead or otherwise occupied.

As he approached the top of the stairs, Jacob crouched. He peeked over the lip, glancing quickly to the left and right. To his left, one man retreated through the doorway into the tower. To his right, another jihadist was just pulling the pin out of a grenade and was about to toss it at the entrance of the gate.

Jacob took him out with a single shot. The man, a skinny guy with his face hidden, staggered back and toppled off the back side of the wall, the grenade going with him and exploding inside the fort.

Jacob winced. He hoped that hadn't hurt any of his comrades.

He sprinted for the doorway to the tower, the arched entrance nothing but a black outline in contrast to the glaring flames at the gate below him and the many lights that had come on inside the fort.

A movement on the turret's parapet caught his eye, and then he was out of sight at its base. He ducked through the doorway and found nothing but a spiral staircase going up to the top of the tower.

There had been one man up there when they had charged. Was he still alive and so there were now two?

He paused, trying to discern sounds above from the rattle of fire echoing through the fort.

He heard nothing, until he heard the *clink clink clink* of a grenade rolling down the stone steps in front of him.

*** 

Jana and the helicopter pilot Antoine sat in the chopper, restless and on edge, as the sounds of battle could be heard distinctly across the clear desert air from five miles away. Occasionally the radio crackled with an update of the battle in progress, but these were vague. When a battle was on, no one really knew what the hell was happening.

Antoine sat in front, while Jana sat in back next to the door gun, a .50 cal machine gun that could really contribute to the fight going on at the fort. Orders were to stay put, however. The team couldn't afford to have the chopper shot down. They'd be stuck in the desert for hours without help, and in that time the jihadists could call in reinforcements and wipe them out.

"You all right back there?" Antione asked in French. She had already impressed the guys with her fluency in the language.

"I wish I could get in on the action," she replied.

As soon as she said this, she wondered if it was true. She hated fighting, hated that it was often necessary. Most of all, she hated the fact that she was good at it. That stupid lecture her father had given about "the mathematics of power" came back to her.

"You and me both," Antoine replied. "The worst part about being a flyboy is I often get left behind. They rib me about it, but I've saved their asses more than once."

"Every member of the team has his role to play," she said, repeating a line her father had often said.

"Or her role. Once we get those artifacts, you can get to work. I've always found archaeology fascinating. I grew up in Nimes. There's a Roman amphitheater and temple right in the middle of town. I used to walk by it every day and dreamed of being an archaeologist."

"Uh-huh."

Jana had been to Nimes and yes, those two monuments were some of the best preserved in the Roman world. But she didn't believe that line about his childhood dreams. Not the way he was looking at her.

He eased out of the pilot's seat and moved back to where she sat by the door gun.

43

"Is it true you've been on missions before?" he asked.

"Yeah. Don't you remember the briefing?"

"Why would the CIA hire an archaeologist?"

Despite the hungry look he was giving her, she had to smile. "You wouldn't believe how many global terror threats have involved archaeological artifacts lately. Shouldn't you be in the pilot's seat?"

He tapped his helmet. "I got a comm link."

He edged closer. She edged away.

"So … that American."

"What about him?" Jana asked.

"Are you and he … "

"Yes."

"Oh." Even with his helmet and dark goggles half obscuring his face, she could see his disappointment. Then he smiled. "I promise not to tell."

He put a hang on her thigh. She slapped it away.

"Back off!"

"But—"

"Back. Off."

Antoine's lips went tight. "Don't give me that. I saw you staring at me in the briefing room."

That was true. He was startlingly attractive, although getting less attractive by the second.

"I was gauging your professionalism."

"You saw how I fly. I can make you fly too."

He reached an arm around her. Jana punched him in the solar plexus. Hard. Unlike the ground team, he wasn't wearing Kevlar and the blow made him double over, clutching his chest and coughing.

"What the hell? You don't have to be so—"

His words were cut off when a gunshot snapped out of the desert night and hit him in the helmet, making him fall limp onto the floor of the helicopter.

# CHAPTER EIGHT

Jacob leapt out of the tower doorway and threw himself around the corner, pressing himself into the narrow space between the doorway and the crenellations of the old French fort's wall. If that grenade rolled out the doorway, he'd be a dead man.

There was a loud bang, and fragments of the doorway's edge snapped off, but none of the shards hit him.

The grenade had detonated at the bottom of the stairs.

The jihadists who had rolled it down the spiral staircase would be checking on him in the next second or two. He had to act fast.

He pulled out a fragmentation grenade, yanked out the pin, and heaved it straight up and onto the top of the tower, which thankfully was less than ten feet above him.

A shout and a bang, and then Jacob was pelting up the spiral staircase and to the top of the tower.

He found one jihadist in a bloody, moaning heap, the other staggering around the small space, trying to hold his face together.

Jacob took them both out with two efficient shots.

A bullet hummed near his ear, close enough for him to hear it even over the ringing caused by the grenade.

He ducked low, getting below the crenellations of the tower's top.

Where had that come from? The battle raged below, but the defenders were so occupied down there that he doubted any had enough time to notice him.

It must have been from one of the other towers.

He crawled to the parapet and dared a peek over.

Only to fall on his ass as a bullet clanked off his Kevlar helmet.

"Damn!"

At least he knew where the shooter was. The only tower that had been visible from his vantage point was the other tower flanking the front gate.

Jacob edged over to the next space between the crenellations and popped up, sending out a three-round burst at his opponent, who was similarly hunkered down between the protective teeth of stone.

45

He missed, and the shooter barely missed him, his bullet ricocheting off the stone by Jacob's head.

*Good shot. Lucky thing he was shooting at something else while I was along the catwalk, otherwise I'd be dog meat.*

The tower was too far to heave a grenade, and he didn't have a grenade launcher.

He popped up again a moment later, firing another three-round burst. Once again he missed and the enemy, barely so.

Getting back down, Jacob gritted his teeth with frustration. How the hell was he going to get this guy? He was savvy and a frighteningly good shot. Plus he had Jacob pinned down in this tower. If he tried going back out the doorway and onto the catwalk, he'd be dead in a heartbeat.

He had no choice but to try what had failed twice before.

Jacob decided not to switch places. He'd shown himself at the same spot twice. A reasonable person would shift position, but no one had ever accused him of being reasonable.

Hopefully the jihadist had a better estimate of him than Jana.

Weird how thoughts of her kept popping up at the most inopportune times. It was almost as if he was obsessed with her or something.

He rose and was surprised to see the jihadist standing, arms flailing. Jacob was just about to pull the trigger when he saw why.

The guy was being dragged backwards while one of the legionnaires slit his throat.

Jacob grinned. "Who says the French can't fight?"

Jacob crawled over to the other side of the tower and peeked over the parapet. He checked out the back towers and saw no movement there. Inside the compound, the French had pushed the jihadists back, taking over most of the grounds, which were littered with dead bodies and collapsed tents. A few jihadists were running away to the far corners of the compound, while fire came from a small stone building near the back that was probably once the commander's quarters.

It looked like a last stand. The artifacts must be in that building.

He hoped the French Foreign Legion guys remembered they were dealing with radioactive material here.

And that gave him a terrible thought. If the Eternal Jihad knew they were going down tonight, would they unsheathe the Staff of Ra and expose everyone in the fort?

He glanced at the dosimeter badge pinned to his Kevlar vest. It didn't show any signs of radiation exposure.

Yet.

He checked the other towers again and didn't see any sign of jihadists. The guy who had saved his ass was firing down on the little building, where from a pair of little square windows the jihadists fired back at the advancing Frenchmen.

The attackers were in a tricky spot. That building looked pretty solid. The jihadists could hold out for a while. And Jacob's side couldn't simply blast it with the rocket launcher because that would risk spreading U-235 all over the inside of the fort, and all over them.

A few seconds later, a couple of legionnaires solved that problem. They appeared on top of one of the back towers, much closer to the building than Jacob's position. One tossed a grenade onto the slate roof, blasting a hole in it and sending shards of slate everywhere. Then his buddy threw a stun grenade through the hole.

That was all the invitation Jacob needed. He sprinted down the stairs and onto the catwalk. The French were already advancing as the guys on the tower threw another couple of stun grenades inside the building. He hurried to catch up with them.

By the time he made it down into the compound and past the scattered fires, dead bodies, and ruined campground to the building, it was all over. The French had mopped up the jihadists inside, finding the half a dozen who had made it into the building unconscious and heavily wounded.

What they didn't find was any artifacts. Jacob took a quick look around. Radio. Maps. A couple of laptops. A bunkbed. Nothing else. He could see without looking that nothing of the dimensions of the Staff of Ra could be hidden here, not to mention all the other boxes of loot they had taken from the Louvre.

Jacob started stomping along the dirt floor, looking for hidden cavities. Maybe there was a dirt-covered hatch leading to a basement or something. A couple of the other guys got the same idea and started stomping as well, while another legionnaire started tapping on the walls.

Nothing.

Captain Vincent swore.

"Fan out around the fort! Establish a perimeter and then search every millimeter of this place!"

One of the jihadists, now all tied up and set along the back wall of the building, let out a moan and shifted his body a little.

Jacob went up to him and addressed him in Arabic. Actually he shouted at him, both because he was pissed off and because the guy had just experienced a stun grenade go off in the same room as him.

"Where are they?"

"Where are what?"

"Don't get coy with me. Where are the artifacts you plundered from the Louvre?"

The jihadist focused bleary eyes on him.

"What are you talking about?"

"We've monitored your chatter. We know about the delivery from France."

"The passports?"

Jacob cocked his head. "What passports?"

"Youssef brought them," the jihadist pointed his chin toward the table where the radio sat. One of the legionnaires nearby, who apparently understood Arabic, opened the table's little drawer, and pulled out a dozen French passports.

The jihadist glanced at his comrades, still lying unconscious beside him.

"I … I don't want to die. We were planning an attack inside France. We sent Youssef, who is a French citizen, to get them. A bunch of us were going to go next week. I'll tell you all about the details and our contacts in the country if you let me live."

"Which one is Youssef?"

He poked his chin at the man at the far end of the line, a hefty, clean-shaven fellow wearing a singed djellaba and with blood trickling out both his shattered eardrums. He must have been right next to the flash bang when it went off.

"Looks like you made yourself a deal. What about the Louvre?"

"Why do you keep asking about the Louvre?"

"You hit the Louvre and took some artifacts. Where are they?"

The jihadist shook his head. "No we didn't. I never even heard about that."

Jacob stared into his eyes, and got the terrible feeling that the terrorist was telling the truth.

\*\*\*

Jana cursed and grabbed the door gun, flicking off the safety just as more shots rang out. Muzzle flares flickered in the dark desert night,

48

appearing to come from about a hundred yards away. Bullets panged off the metal side of the chopper. One passed through the doorway right by her shoulder to ricochet around the interior.

She opened up with the door gun, the rounds pouring out of the weapon in a rapid *thud thud thud*. She'd never used one before and was poor at aiming, but the sheer storm of lead she sent in the attackers' direction stopped their firing as they all dove for cover.

That wouldn't last long. One of those jihadists might have a rocket-propelled grenade. This raid would be over pretty quick if he did.

Jana fired for a few more seconds, grabbed Romeo, and hauled him out of sight. Then she got back on the door gun and sprayed the area for a few more seconds.

Hoping that would buy her enough time, she clambered to the front of the helicopter and got in the cockpit.

Now came the tough part. She'd never flown a helicopter. Her dad had bought her a simulator and she'd flown all sorts of helicopters and aircraft with it—part of Aaron Peters's mixture of play and training—but she'd never actually sat in a cockpit.

No time like the present. The chopper was already powered up, and so she strapped in, switched on the rotors, and tried to do her best.

Her best turned out not very good. The Pentagon-made simulator, which had been the most fun video game Jana had played as a kid, way more realistic and high-tech than the Nintendo 64 or the early PlayStation, couldn't reproduce the deep vibration of the machine, the sudden jerk as it took off and tilted forward, or the stress of hearing bullets panging off the metal sides.

The ground tilted up toward her as she angled too far forward. Jana overcompensated and saw nothing but the sky. She fought panic and managed to level out. She hovered for a moment, wobbling precariously.

Now she had to gain altitude and get to the fort.

The problem was, she could barely see anything. Antoine still wore his helmet with the electronic readouts and IR capability. All she saw was a dark desert and a starry sky above. At least those guys down below weren't shooting any RPGs at her.

The streak of a rocket right in front of her window proved that assumption wrong. Jana yelped and moved forward and up, overcompensating again and nearly sending the chopper hurtling into the sand. This chopper was a different make than the ones she had trained on with the simulator as a teen, fifteen years ago. Briefly she

49

wondered if Antoine was still back there or if he had tumbled out of the open door. She had forgotten to strap him in.

Now where was that fort?

Bullets hitting the chopper reminded her of a more immediate problem. She hit some extra power to gain more altitude. This chopper was equipped with an arsenal of weaponry, but she hadn't been trained on any of it and didn't want to risk a maneuver to engage with the forces on the ground.

Another rocket streaked past, cutting a flaming trail through the night. Jana increased speed and wobbled out of range.

Now completely disoriented, she had no idea which way the fort lay. She gained more altitude and performed a slow, cautious circle. About halfway through the maneuver she spotted a red glare in the distance.

*If something's on fire in the desert, it's probably Jacob's fault.*

She headed for it.

In a matter of minutes the fort came into clear view. She saw flames in several places, but no gunfire. She made a low pass and saw several of the Frenchmen waving up at her, no doubt wondering why Antoine had flown here and why he wasn't responding to radio calls. She pulled a little distance away, licked her lips, tried to relax, and began to land. She had never been good at landings.

Slowly. Slowly. The desert floor, garishly lit by the flames in the fort, was at least visible. Even so, she came down too fast, and the impact when the helicopter hit the earth was almost enough to send her through the roof. Jacob and a couple of legionnaires rushed over.

She cut the rotors and climbed back to the rear of the chopper, relieved to find Antoine still lying crumpled among the gear. She felt even more relief when he moaned and held his head. She didn't see any blood. The helmet had saved him. He had only been knocked out.

Jacob came running up. "What happened?"

"Ambush. Must have been a patrol from Eternal Jihad. Did you recover the Staff of Ra?"

Jacob shook his head grimly. "We got the wrong group. The shipment the French intercepted chatter about turned out to be French passports. They were planning a hit within the country."

Jana groaned and sat down, looking out over the desert, where to the east the first faint light of dawn was coloring the black sky a deep blue. She checked her watch.

The deadline had nearly passed, and they had no idea what the thieves would do once it did.

# CHAPTER NINE

*Giza, Egypt*
*Three hours later ...*

Harvey Goldman was having the time of his life. He'd always wanted to visit Egypt and see the pyramids, and now, one month into retirement, here he was!

He and his wife Ethel stood just inside the entrance, where they had arrived first thing so they could get in before the crowds.

That hadn't worked out so well. A dozen tour buses had been waiting there with them.

It didn't matter, though, because the people swarming around the site were like ants compared to the three immense monuments towering before them.

Right in front of them stood the Great Pyramid of Khufu, the first pyramid to be built on the Giza plateau around 2570 BC. The age of the thing, and its sheer size, boggled the mind. Nearby stood the Pyramid of Khafre, which still had some of its original facing stones near the top, and next to it stood the somewhat smaller but still impressive Pyramid of Menkaure.

He and Ethel would see the inside of every one of them.

"No thank you," Ethel said to an Egyptian man in a white turban and djellaba holding up some colorful guidebooks.

"They tell you all you need to know, madam."

"I have my guidebook right here." Ethel pointed to her husband and laughed.

Harvey smiled proudly. He'd been studying Egyptology for years, a relaxing break from being a tax consultant. Mummies and pharaohs had a bigger attraction for an active mind than tax law.

They walked toward the main event, the Pyramid of Khufu. The small entrance had been hacked out of the side by the British archaeologist Howard Vyse in 1837, about sixty feet above the surface of the desert. People clambered over the big stones to get up to it, helped by a string of Egyptian men in white djellabas hoping for a tip.

When they got close to the base, Harvey and Ethel stopped to take a couple of photographs.

Those photographs saved their lives.

Just as Harvey focused his camera, bought specially for this trip of a lifetime, the ground shook with a detonation. Smoke rose out of the pyramid's entrance, shot out by an incredible force. People standing near the entrance or walking up the side toppled over, falling from one stone to the next, their bodies flopping in unnatural angles. A moment later, there was a loud rumble and more shaking.

Harvey and Ethel gripped each other, too stunned to move.

The dust slowly cleared to reveal the entrance had disappeared. Several ancient stone blocks, each weighing two tons, had tumbled down, crushing anyone nearby and sealing those inside in an eternal tomb.

\*\*\*

Jana felt ill. They were on a French Air Force plane back to Aswan and a satellite video link was relaying the Giza attack. The pyramid of Khufu had been damaged. As far as Egyptian authorities could tell, a suicide bomber had gotten through security and entered the interior passage of the pyramid, which had been packed with tourists. He must have had some C4 packs jammed into a weak point between the stones, because simply blowing himself up would have caused the force of the explosion to blow out the entrance without doing any structural damage.

It had been set perfectly, knocking out a loose stone and causing an avalanche of several other stones, sealing the people inside. Frantic excavation efforts were underway in the hope of finding survivors, but Jana doubted any would still be alive. The shrapnel, the sonic force, and the sheer stampeding panic would have probably killed all of them.

But the real thing that made Jana sick was the irreparable damage done to one of the world's most iconic ancient monuments. She knew it was wrong to feel more for a stone building than actual human beings, but she couldn't help it. Was nothing sacred to these people?

The answer was a resounding no. The video feed showed Egyptian men in some neighborhoods dancing in the streets. These were members of the Muslim Brotherhood, a hardcore Islamist organization that had briefly taken power before the current military junta overthrew them. During their short reign, the mummy room in the Egyptian museum was shut, Egypt's Christian community saw several of their churches burn, and there was open discussion by some clerics of lowering the marriage age to eight.

While most Egyptians were appalled by all of this, there was an unsettled, alienated minority in their country who wanted a strict Islamic regime, and hated the ancient monuments that brought so many decadent Westerners to their nation.

Some of the legionnaires cheered when the video showed Egyptian police hitting the dancers with batons. Jana didn't feel like cheering. The damage had been done and Egypt's tourist economy, which made up the bulk of its hard currency earnings, would be wrecked for years. Those same idiots dancing in the streets would watch their standard of living plunge as Egypt fell into a long recession.

"This is my fault," Jacob said glumly beside her. "We were too quick to go for the obvious culprits."

"Don't blame yourself," Jana said, putting a hand on his arm. "The French thought they had a good lead."

Jacob grunted. "Too obvious. The Sword of the Righteous is smarter than that."

"We're not even sure we're dealing with the Sword of the Righteous."

"That break-in was really well-planned. The hicks we took out in Chad weren't up for it."

"At least we stopped another terror attack," Jana said, "and none of our guys got killed."

The wounded had been shipped out on another plane, including two critical cases. Antoine got off with a concussion. Jana hadn't mentioned the harassment. It didn't matter anymore.

The only thing that mattered was recovering the Staff of Ra before whoever stole it made a dirty bomb. But their only solid lead turned out to be a dead-end.

Now what the hell were they going to do?

*\*\*\**

A remote farm in Denmark seemed like an unusual place to go to buy advanced weaponry, but Aaron Peters had spent most of his adult life in unusual places.

Aaron rode a horse he had rented from a stable in the nearby town of Slagelse along a narrow trail between flat, open fields. Claus Pedersen had a strict rule that if you were buying, you couldn't approach his farm in a vehicle. Rumor had it that his boyfriend had been killed in a car bombing. Aaron had no idea if that was true or not. Most likely he just wanted to have more time to get a good look at any potential customers.

He had, of course, reached out to Pedersen through a trusted intermediary, but it always paid to be careful. Aaron could respect that.

Aaron had already spotted a couple of cameras hidden in fenceposts, and he was sure he was missing at least a couple more.

The farm compound appeared typical for the region—a one-story stone house that looked at least a century old, a wooden stable nearby, and a long building of corrugated steel. As the wind shifted, Aaron caught a whiff of something nasty. Smelled like he kept pigs in there.

No sign of life, though. Aaron hoped Pedersen didn't get trigger happy. Things were getting unsettled in the underworld just like they were in the public world. Who knew what kind of drama he was dealing with.

A stocky man in his fifties walked out of the building of corrugated steel. His blonde hair was long but thinning on top. He wore overalls and dirty Wellingtons and carried a shovel in one hand.

He did not look like the greatest engineering genius the arms industry had ever seen, now working freelance with a strict remit to only sell to the good guys. Many Western intelligence agencies watched him, and many bought from him.

None, however, could buy him. Claus Pedersen had quit his last corporate job ten years ago. Aaron didn't know why and he was quite sure he'd never find out.

The engineer stopped and studied Aaron as he approached, leaning on the shovel.

When Aaron got within a few yards of the gravel courtyard between the three buildings, Pedersen gave a casual gesture.

"Hitch your horse to that post there. Looks like we won't have rain for a while."

Aaron glanced up at the leaden sky. Pedersen really was a farmer as well as many other things. He'd take the Dane's word for it.

Pedersen glanced at his palm, then looked back at him.

"Thanks for following instructions and coming unarmed."

"How do you know that?" Aaron asked, curious more than surprised.

"Those two posts you went through are body scanners."

Pedersen held up a small phone hidden in his broad hand and walked closer so Aaron could get a good look. The screen showed the horse and rider in profile on both sides, and every bit of metal on him, from the coins in his pocket to the metal rods in his leg from reconstructive surgery.

"Wait, what's that thing on my shoulder?"

Pedersen looked at it. "Appears to be some shrapnel."

"Huh. I thought they got it all out."

"Hard to get good help these days. Speaking of, what are you looking for?"

"I heard you have some top-of-the-line drones."

"From what I heard, a man like you can get the best the Pentagon has built."

"I've heard you have better."

Pedersen nodded. "Come on inside. Want some coffee?"

"I'm fine."

The farmer led him into the corrugated steel building. A wide door stood open at one end, and within he saw a series of large stalls on both sides filled with pigs. The stench was ten times worse inside.

Pedersen walked to a stall about two-thirds of the way down the center aisle and opened it.

He turned to Aaron. "You're not Jewish or Muslim, are you?"

"Pigs don't bother me."

"Still, you might want to take off your shoes and put on those." Pedersen indicated a pair of Wellingtons standing next to the stall.

As Pedersen entered, Aaron glanced inside the stall, saw a bunch of pigs rolling and walking around at least a couple of inches of mud and dung, and decided to take the farmer's advice. Then he joined Pedersen in the stall, walking to the back where the man waited for him.

The Wellingtons protected Aaron's feet, but nothing stopped his pants from getting smeared with mire as fat porkers brushed their smelly sides against him. Aaron had dealt with worse, but he wasn't sure how he'd explain his condition to the folks at the stable back in Slagelse.

Pedersen touched the corrugated steel wall in a certain pattern. Aaron squinted and couldn't see any sort of switch, just a few filthy stains in a pattern a bit above the level of the pigs. There was a click and a hum. The pigs moved to the far side of the stall as a portal opened in the floor.

"Pigs are smart," Pedersen explained. "They know not to come close to the opening."

"It doesn't look too dangerous," Aaron said, observing the concrete steps leading down to a lit cellar.

"No, but any pigs that come close get turned into bacon that same day. They've learned this. You like bacon? I'll give you a kilo. The best bacon you've ever tasted."

"Thanks."

They descended the stairs and Aaron beheld an arsenal similar to what arms dealers had hidden under buildings all over the world.

But there was a difference. Instead of racks of AK-47s and bins full of grenades, he saw shelves holding drones of various shapes and sizes. None of them were available commercially, and most were more advanced than the ones the Pentagon could give him.

Which was why he was here.

Beyond the row of shelves, Aaron spotted a workshop with a lathe, drill, soldering iron, and other electronic and mechanical equipment. Claus Pedersen was a lot more than a pig farmer.

"So what are your needs?"

"I'm going up against a technologically savvy and organized opponent. I need speed, stealth, armor-piercing capability, and ease of assembly. Plus I have to make it look innocuous to the average cop or soldier."

"So you're going after a target outside the European Union?"

"Yes. I'll have to pass across borders."

"I thought you always flew private."

"I do, but it pays to be careful."

Orhan would fly him to where he needed to go, but that didn't mean that everyone in the airport where they'd land would take their bribes and mind their own business like they were supposed to.

"How much armor-piercing capability do you need? Tanks? Bunkers?"

"Tanks," Aaron said, "or a similar level of armor."

Actually, he was hitting a limousine, but a limousine armored like a tank. And he might have to go for a reinforced civilian dwelling as well.

"Any size limitations?"

"No, within reason."

"Then I'd suggest my Pedersen Model 86, what I like to call the Flying Pig."

With a dramatic gesture of his calloused hand, Pedersen indicated a hulking drone of black gleaming metal, the biggest in view.

"This fellow is made entirely of plastic and ultra-dense ceramic, even the engine parts, and will not show up on radar. It has twice the speed and range of those cheap American drones you're used to using, and comes supplied with IR and visual imaging equipment plus a rocket launcher with a four-round magazine. The ultracompact rockets come in armor piercing or bunker buster varieties."

"I'll take the bunker busters if they live up to their names."

The arms manufacturer grinned. "Oh, they do. Don't worry about that."

A bunker buster bomb was designed to penetrate armor or walls and detonate once it got through. A normal explosive detonated on impact, which in the case of a strong wall only gouged a crater in it. Bunker busters would drill a hole and blow up anything beyond the barrier.

"How far can they penetrate?"

"Any main battle tank and up to three feet of reinforced concrete. Good enough?"

Aaron took a deep breath. "Good enough."

*Good enough if I can get to the target without The Order discovering my plans. Good enough if I can get to the target site alive. Good enough if they don't have effective countermeasures.*

*Nothing is ever good enough. But I've got to keep fighting.*

# CHAPTER TEN

"It's unacceptable!" Monsieur Dubois shouted, shaking his fists in the air as he paced around his classical-style office complete with imitation Greek statues of nude goddesses. One of them had the same cup size as Dubois's mistress, Tyler noticed. Perhaps he should inform Madame Dubois of that.

Working on sensitive issues for the federal government, Tyler Wallace was accustomed to getting chewed out when circumstances beyond his control didn't give the politicians what they hoped for.

The French had acted on their own intel, with mostly their own men, and asked Jacob and Jana to go along for their expertise.

The failure was a French failure, but Monsieur Dubois, head of the Direction générale de la Sécurité extérieure, was blaming it all on him. Probably because his next meeting was with the French president.

"Unacceptable!" the man repeated, in case Tyler hadn't heard him screaming at jet engine decibels. "We take out the wrong terrorist group, and a pyramid gets attacked! Even worse, because the Egyptian government was in on the raid, now they're blaming us for the blowback. This is a disaster for our relations in North Africa. It will have ripple effects on trade and border controls and intelligence gathering. Egyptian intelligence leaks like a sieve. Half the governments in the Sahel probably know of your failure by now. All our diplomatic and military efforts will be set back a decade!"

Tyler decided not to correct the man about whose fault it was. Instead, he pointed out the obvious in the hope that it would bring Dubois back down to Earth.

"Of greater and more immediate concern is the fact that this terror cell is still free to operate. And from the chatter we've received relating to The Sword of the Righteous, there is no indication that they did it."

"They're keeping silent."

"Perhaps."

"At least silent to each other, not to us."

"The thieves got in contact?"

"Yes. A new deadline. Forty-eight hours or they'll launch another attack."

"Did they say of what nature?"

"Of course not, just that we have forty-eight hours. If we don't comply, they'll strike again. Oh, and the ransom has gone up to 1.5 billion euros."

*Close to two billion U.S. dollars. Wonderful.*

Tyler considered their options.

"What's your government's stance on paying the ransom?"

"A bad precedent," Dubois said, sitting down hard in his leather armchair and suddenly looking tired. He ran a hand through thinning hair. "Plus there's no guarantee they won't simply attack their next target anyway. And don't call it a ransom. They're not promising to return the objects in exchange for the money; they're simply demanding money."

"So there won't be a payout."

"I didn't say that. We're negotiating through an intermediary, a Muslim cleric in Beirut. We're trying to get some concessions on our end, like at least a return of everything stolen except the Staff of Ra. They've already said the staff wouldn't be negotiable."

"And the other objects are?"

"Perhaps."

"What other leads has your intel come up with? So far, we at the CIA haven't found anything."

Dubois gave him a sharp look. "The CIA has been less than helpful in this crisis."

"Have you come up with any intel?" Tyler tried very hard not to put any emphasis on the "you."

The answer was what he expected.

"No. We don't have anything. They seemed to have come out of nowhere."

"No one this well-trained comes out of nowhere."

"True, but we've run the sketches through facial recognition software and haven't come up with any matches for known or suspected terrorists, or even petty criminals."

"We'll put all our resources into this," Tyler reassured him. "The British and Germans have promised their support as well, and of course the Egyptians. We'll find them."

"We better," Dubois muttered. "Because if they hit the Great Pyramid of Giza, I can't imagine what they'll do for an encore."

\*\*\*

60

Jana sat in the ops room of an Egyptian army base in the Sahara desert fifty miles west of Aswan. She, Jacob, Captain Vincent, and a whole team of Egyptian intelligence officers worked feverishly, trying to figure out where the shadowy terrorist group would strike next. They had all heard about the second deadline, and were all equally lost as to where the next attack would take place.

Jana suspected it would not be in Egypt. Tourists were in such a rush to get out of the country that airlines had added extra flights to accommodate them all. Leave had been canceled for all security personnel and every tourist site had been shut down. The military had declared martial law, rounded up any radicals they hadn't already put in prison, and conducted scores of raids on suspect terror cells and criminal gangs.

The government was casting their net wide, but neither she nor Jacob thought they'd catch the real culprits that way. The best they could hope for were similar results to the raid the French Foreign Legion had just conducted—catching real terrorists but not the right terrorists.

"Intelligence work is meticulous work," her father always used to say. "Results often take a lot of time."

The problem was, they didn't have a lot of time. The barely had any time.

Jacob was scrolling through the latest intel on The Sword of the Righteous. An SAS team had hit one of their cells in Nigeria and wiped them out. The terrorists had gone down fighting and didn't offer the Brits any prisoners. MI6 was currently going through a couple of laptops they'd recovered there, but had yet to find anything valuable. The group had made an announcement on the usual Dark Web sites, lauding the Giza attack but not claiming responsibility.

"Maybe I had it all wrong," he kept muttering.

Jana worried about him. He was taking this setback hard, even though it wasn't anyone's fault. The French had been right to go after that splinter group; the intel looked promising, so it wasn't their fault either or certainly not Jacob's. She wondered if Aaron leaving again had something to do with his mood. He had been as close to him as she had.

*Closer.*

She tamped down her habitual jealousy. There was no time for that right now. Besides, her mind was trying to tell her something,

61

something she had read a while back but hadn't stuck because it hadn't seemed relevant.

Now it did. The urgency of trying to recall it hinted at that. Obviously her subconscious thought it might be of value.

But what the hell was it?

A room full of men talking urgently in Arabic, French, and English, along with phones ringing all the time, was hardly conducive to remembering something on the tip of her tongue. She got up and walked out. Jacob was so intent on the SAS action report that he didn't even notice.

After going down a short hallway, she exited a door flanked by a pair of guards and walked out into the compound. Although fully lit, she could still see some stars in the crystal clear desert night. She stood looking at them for a moment, trying to clear her mind.

She felt eyes on her and looked over her shoulder. The guards were staring at her. Fine. Let them stare. Working as a woman in the Middle East she had grown accustomed to staring. Unlike that idiot Antoine, these guys at least seemed professional enough not to leave their posts.

Jana looked back up at the stars. Museum. It had something to do with a museum. Or something in a museum newsletter she subscribed to.

What? She pulled out her phone, which was linked to the military Wi-Fi here at the base, and opened up the latest issue of *Museum News*.

In that strange way memory works, she remembered just as she hit the attachment on her email.

An employee of the British Museum in London had been murdered the previous month. She scrolled down to the article and read the obituary.

Frederick Caldwell had been an assistant curator of Egyptology at the museum, helping to oversee one of the greatest Egyptian collections in Europe. But more than that, he was a private collector. Born into wealth, he had taken on both avocations out of pure enthusiasm. Caldwell had been good at his work too, unlike many rich people who dabble in science. He had published several academic papers and had been well-respected in the field.

The article, and an article she found in a London newspaper, said Frederick Caldwell had been walking near his house late one night, supposedly going home, when he had been stabbed to death. His keys had been stolen and a number of items taken from his residence. No witnesses, no clear CCTV images, and no arrests.

Jana wished she knew more about him aside from this brief article and a few things she'd heard through the grapevine. Her specialty was Roman archaeology. Jacob seemed to think she could answer any question relating to any ancient culture in the world. It didn't work like that. There was too much knowledge for one person to know.

But she didn't need to be an Egyptologist to know that the murder of someone at a prominent museum, an Egyptologist and collector at that, might have a link to the Louvre break-in. The more she learned about the secret world that manipulated the more visible one, the less she believed in coincidences.

Jana went back inside. The two guards smiled at her and said something in Arabic which she didn't bother to listen to.

Jacob was still looking through MI6 reports.

"Do you have a good contact with that agency?" she asked, gesturing to the screen.

"Sure. Plenty."

"Can they get access to a police report in London and send it to us?"

"No problem," he was already typing a request to someone at MI6's London headquarters. "Give me the details."

"It's about a collector who worked at the British Museum's Egyptology department. He got murdered last month and his home broken into."

Jacob looked up at her for a second, eyes going wide, then got back to typing.

"I'll label this priority."

# CHAPTER ELEVEN

For what must have been the thousandth time, Jacob was glad Jana Peters had come along on the mission. The police report on the murder of Frederick Caldwell and the break-in of his home had yielded a mother lode of interesting information.

CCTV footage in his exclusive neighborhood of Holland Park in central London showed Caldwell had been stabbed to death by three hooded figures who came at him from different angles, all at the same time. While they had taken his wallet and keys, that had obviously been only a cover to make it look like a typical mugging. The coordinated way these three moved in on him, and the fact that they didn't pause to demand his wallet before poking him full of holes, proved this to be a hit.

There was no CCTV close to his residence, so everything had to be reconstructed at that point. Police had found a bloodstain on a baseboard in the front hall of the residence that matched Caldwell's DNA, no doubt left there from a bloodstain on one of the intruder's pants. Inside, Caldwell had an exhibition room for his prize objects and several other items on display in various other rooms.

Two large items were missing from the exhibition room, and a few smaller items were missing from other rooms. This was evident from dust marks on the shelves and blank spots on the wall.

Caldwell was in the habit of posting labels next to each item. These had been removed as well. His laptop was also missing, which presumably contained a database of his collection. No hard copy was found. Reconstructing the arrangement from rather vague explanations from his friends, a large inscription in hieroglyphs was missing as well as a bas-relief showing Egyptian gods. Several small statuettes were missing too. No further detail.

"Why aren't the witnesses being more specific? You'd think his collector cronies would know all about this stuff," Jacob wondered aloud.

"Look at the description of the witnesses," Jana pointed out. "Retired barrister. Accountant. Physician. There isn't a single

64

archaeologist or historian in the bunch. And I bet there isn't a single collector either."

"That's weird."

"Or significant. It looks like he didn't want his collection studied by anyone who knew what they were looking at."

"What was he hiding?"

"His murderers know."

"Maybe his boss at the museum knows too?"

"Maybe. Look how vague the interview is that he gave to the police. Claims never to have been to his house or socialized with him after work. From what I've read, Frederick Caldwell was a social butterfly. He was a member of three different exclusive Pall Mall clubs and several professional organizations. He was a regular at academic conferences and collectors' fairs."

"Looks like we should go to London."

"A seven-hour flight on a hunch?" Jana said, suddenly unsure of herself.

Jacob grinned. "Your hunches generally turn into good leads. And I think you're right, I don't think the next hit will be in Egypt. No one can get anywhere near an ancient site at the moment, and the tourists are all leaving."

"Let's get on the next flight then."

***

At midmorning London time, a yawning Jana and Jacob made it to their appointment with the head of the British Museum and the head of the Egyptology Department, Drs. Henley and Burford.

Jana noted that the two couldn't be more different. Henley, the museum director, was a man of trim middle-age in an expensive suit. Jana imagined him meeting and greeting big donors at fancy London clubs. She'd met his type before. Useful but annoying, and often condescending.

Dr. Burford, the Egyptologist, was a hunched and mumbling older man in an old and ill-fitting suit. Henley looked guarded, with a plastered-on smile more suitable to a politician, while Burford looked like he hadn't slept in a week.

They met in Henley's office, on the top floor of the museum with a sweeping view of the red brick Victorian spires and more sedate gray stone Georgian dwellings of Bloomsbury. Someone from MI6 had

65

made a call requesting this interview. Jana got the impression it wouldn't have happened otherwise.

"We will of course help American intelligence in any way possible," Henley said after his young and exceptionally lovely secretary had set down tea for four and closed the door behind her. "The break-in at the Louvre is tragic, simply tragic."

"Nothing compared to Giza," Burford whispered with a haunted look.

Jana nodded in sympathy, trying, and failing to catch the old man's eye.

"What can you tell us about Frederick Caldwell?" Jacob asked.

Henley shifted in his seat. "Another tragedy. I don't know what's happening to this city. So much riffraff causing trouble."

"Do you know anyone who would wish him harm?"

"No one. He was obviously targeted for his collection, but it's curious. They didn't need to kill him, and they didn't take some of the most valuable pieces."

"Are you familiar with his collection?" Jana asked.

"No. I was never invited to his home."

"Neither was I," added Burford. "And I dropped no shortage of hints. It seems strange. He was otherwise quite open and friendly."

"So if neither of you saw the collection, how do you know the thieves didn't take some of the most valuable pieces?"

"We were both brought in by the police to examine the house," Burford said. "In his display room he had an extremely rare Predynastic frieze, and in his living room a beautiful head of a princess from the Second Intermediate Period, the paint marvelously preserved. Either one of those would be the high point of any private collection. I cannot imagine the thieves would have overlooked such fine work if they knew what they were doing. And if they didn't know what they were doing, they would have taken the gold figurines in his bedroom and display room."

Jana sat back and considered this for a moment. MI6 had sent them the police report. There had been no solid leads, and since all of Caldwell's records had been stolen, the police had no clear idea what he had purchased or whom he had purchased it from.

"Do you have any idea where he bought his antiquities?" Jana asked.

Henley shook his head. Burford spoke up.

"About a week ago, I finally got around to cleaning out his desk. A painful task that I kept putting off. I was really quite fond of the man. His next of kin have shown far more interest in his bank account than any personal items. Frederick had no close relations. I didn't find much in his desk, but I did find a card for Eastern Antiquities. It's an antiquities dealer not far from here. I telephoned the police but I don't know if they've followed it up."

Jana and Jacob exchanged a look. The police hadn't followed up. It wasn't in the report, and with the police being overworked, they probably hadn't gotten around to it.

Jana decided they should remedy that.

*** 

Eastern Antiquities was set on a side street just beyond Bedford Square, one of the best preserved 18th century squares in London. Jana had often admired the orderly rows of old houses in the evenings after visiting the museum, and she had even passed Eastern Antiquities, but had never entered.

Jana held an archaeologist's dislike of the antiquities trade. While all dealers had to abide by strict rules of provenance, the trade was rife with clever forgeries and stolen goods. Was it any surprise that after the invasion of Iraq, the antiquities shops suddenly had a lot more Sumerian and Babylonian artifacts? Or when the revolution in Egypt kicked off, there were suddenly more Egyptian antiquities?

Still, she couldn't help but look admiringly at the window display as they pressed the buzzer to be allowed entry. Three shelves greeted her. The bottom one held a stone head of an Old Kingdom pharaoh, a bit battered but still a choice find. Next to it was a set of four Canopic jars that made Jana think of the first adventure she'd gone on with the fascinating and irritating man beside her. On the middle shelf were several shabtis, faience figurines that were placed in Egyptian tombs to act as servants in the afterlife. Next to them were several Sumerian figurines of men and women carved in ivory, with huge eyes and pleading hands, praying to their stern gods. On the top shelf she admired various gold and silver pieces of jewelry from Egypt, Babylonia, and the Hittite civilization of Anatolia.

"No price tags," Jacob said. "If you have to ask, you can't afford it."

The door buzzed and they entered, to be greeted by an elegant elderly gentleman with swept-back white hair and wearing a red velvet smoking jacket and slippers, complete with fez.

Despite the faux Eastern attire, he looked and spoke like a blue-blooded Englishman.

"How may I help you today?"

Jacob pulled out an ID Jana had seen him use before.

"We're with Interpol. We're investigating the murder of Frederick Caldwell."

The man looked uncertain. "I … see. Such a terrible thing. May I examine your identification?"

"Sure." Jacob handed it over. Whatever this man might know about Interpol IDs, it would certainly pass muster. The CIA's forgeries division did excellent work, or maybe it was a real Interpol ID and Jacob worked for them too. Who knew? It troubled her that what she knew about the man she had fallen in love with was dwarfed by what she didn't know.

The antiquities dealer returned the ID and turned to Jana. "And your identification, madam?"

"I don't have it with me."

"Then I'm afraid—"

"You're going to answer our questions, or our investigation will take on a new angle," Jacob snapped.

The man turned back to him with an irritated expression. He obviously wasn't accustomed to being talked to in such a fashion, but when he saw the hard glint in Jacob's eye, and his gaze flicked over the CIA agent's physique, he blinked rapidly, put back on his fake smile and said, "Come into my office."

As they sat in a wood-paneled office on leather armchairs, the walls decorated with old prints and a page from a French illuminated manuscript, Jana got right to the point.

"I have a background in archaeology and I need to know precisely what Frederick Caldwell purchased from you."

After the briefest of hesitation, the man replied, "He bought several items over the years. I can't give you a list or show you photographs because he made me destroy my files."

"Destroy your files?" Jana asked. "Why?"

"He got a bit cagey when I asked him that. He said he wanted complete privacy. He claimed he had other collectors bothering him before about buying items from his collection and was worried about theft."

"So you agreed to destroy your files?" Jacob asked. "Isn't that a violation of tax law?"

"I kept the receipts and the list in my accounting program," the man said in a tone of haughty defensiveness. "I am aware that it's an unusual step, but he was a valued client and I kept all documentation necessary to stay within government regulations. I maintain the highest standards of legality here."

*Yeah, sure you do.*

Jana decided not to say that. He had enough barriers up already.

"So what did he buy? There were a couple of larger pieces, probably from a temple or tomb. One was an inscription and another showed various gods, probably with an accompanying inscription."

"I remember those clearly. Both were from northern Sudan, possibly from the same temple due to the similarities in style and material. It's unclear because they were excavated by a French team in the late 1800s. As you know, archaeologists did not keep the best of records at that time, and many records were lost in the war. One panel was an extensive hieroglyphic inscription and the other showed the pharaoh Senusret III making offerings to Ra."

*Ra again.*

"Was Ra carrying a staff?"

The antiquities dealer cocked his head at this seemingly odd question. "Why, yes. I do believe he was. Why, have you found it?"

"The staff or the panel?" Jana asked.

The antiquities dealer laughed. "The panel, of course. Please don't tell me you believe in that old tale."

"Of course not," Jana smiled. "Just a joke."

Actually a probe. She wanted to see his reaction. The laughter had reached his eyes, so unless he was an actor as well as an antiquities dealer, he wasn't involved any more than he appeared to be.

Jacob cut in. "Wait, they found them in the Sudan? I thought they were Egyptian."

The elderly gentlemen let out a little chuckle, and in a condescending voice explained, "The Sudan was conquered several times by Egypt in antiquity, although just as often the Nubians would break away again. The pharaoh Senusret III conducted an extensive campaign of conquest south of Aswan. The Egyptians wanted access to the Nubian gold and slave market."

69

Jacob looked about to give an angry response. Jana cut him off. "What other items did you sell him?"

"Oh, various things. The head of a princess. An exquisite predynastic frieze. Quite a find. Stone and bronze statuettes of various Egyptian deities."

"Including Ra?"

"Yes, several of the sun god."

"And where did you purchase these items from?"

"Oh, many different sources, both in Africa and Europe."

"Where in Africa?"

"Egypt and the Sudan. He exclusively collected artifacts from that region."

"Any in France?"

Again the curious look. "Why, yes. Les Frères Michaux have been a major source. They have the best antiquities dealership in Paris."

"Thank you for your help," Jana said.

*Looks like our next stop is Paris.*

# CHAPTER TWELVE

Jacob felt left behind in all this discussion of ancient artifacts and civilizations. He had never been big on history and it hadn't exactly been a priority in his Ranger and CIA training. Driving a rental car into central Paris that evening, he asked Jana to fill him in.

"I've been too focused on the uranium in the Staff of Ra and haven't asked you about the legend behind it. What can you tell me?"

Jana looked out at the beautiful buildings they passed, seemingly so peaceful and yet all under threat of a dirty bomb. Even worse, Jacob couldn't help but remember the even greater threat her father had warned them of.

Could The Order be behind all this? Aaron Peters had said they tried to cause disruption wherever they could. Perhaps the terrorist groups were their puppets, maybe without even realizing it.

Jana spoke.

"We all heard about the Staff of Ra when going through university. It never made it big in the public eye, which is surprising considering how much the public likes conspiracy theories. Maybe it was too obtuse. The story goes that the Staff of Ra was given by the sun god to the high priest at Karnak as an emblem of his might, and as a weapon to assert imperial authority. The priest was generally from the royal family, and the priesthood and the pharaoh worked hand in hand. It was called the 'withering power of Ra' and supposedly the priest would use it to blast invaders or enemies of the state."

"With that uranium in it, the priest would get blasted too, as would everyone else," Jacob said, taking a turn onto the road that would take them to their hotel right next to the Louvre. The CIA usually didn't splash out for five stars, but they needed to be right in the area of operations and there were no cheap hotels next to the Louvre.

"Sure, just like that Canopic jar. Open it and everyone suffers a lingering death. Maybe the priest didn't mind since he'd be blessed in the afterlife. Or maybe the staff had some sort of focusing device."

"What, like an X-ray machine?" Jacob asked. "The ancients couldn't project radiation."

71

Jana shrugged. "Maybe they could. Two years ago, everyone thought the ancients didn't know what radiation was."

"Good point. So if there was a focusing device, maybe the thieves are after that too."

"Yeah, but nothing that snob in Bloomsbury told us about sounds like a focusing device," Jana said.

"Maybe the thieves made another hit, or maybe they're not done yet. So who's this Senusret III guy?"

"A pharaoh of the Middle Kingdom. He ruled from 1878 BC to 1839 BC. His grandfather, Senusret I, conquered northern Nubia after it had been free of Egyptian influence for a long time. Senusret III expanded the conquest and built a string of forts to protect the new border."

"Maybe the Staff of Ra was used to fight off the Nubians?"

"There's no record of that, but maybe. Except the Staff of Ra was kept at the temple of Karnak in Luxor, hundreds of miles to the north."

"Huh. Well, whatever they did with it, I'm a bit more concerned about what our Islamist friends will do with it. If they get that focusing device, it could be a seriously dangerous weapon, potentially worse than a dirty bomb because it could be used more than once. It would have to be some sort of heavy lead container with some sort of device to focus and project the radiation."

"What would that be?"

"No idea. Maybe like a lens or something. What's the word? A collimator. They use it in radiotherapy, don't they? To be honest, I don't know how it works in the modern world. Who knows how the ancients did it."

"Maybe the director of the Louvre has some idea."

That's where they were headed right now. Given how he hadn't revealed the existence of this potentially dangerous artifact until it was stolen, they had decided to pay him a surprise visit.

Les Frères Michaux had already closed. If they didn't get any good answers from the Louvre director, they'd go to the antiquities dealer and see what they could provide.

Jacob looked at his watch and tapped his thumb on the steering wheel. The forty-eight hour deadline was ticking away fast. They had twenty-six hours left before the thieves made another terror strike.

What if the next was the big one? What if they already had everything they needed? They sure did for a dirty bomb, and maybe they were a step ahead of him and Jana and already had the focusing device, assuming it had existed and had survived the millennia.

Too many uncertainties. They'd have to get that museum director to talk or else.

Jacob had gone through the files on Henri Etienne on the flight from London. While the French police didn't suspect him of any wrongdoing, given the seriousness of the crime and its subsequent fallout, they were sharing all the information they had on anyone even remotely connected to the case.

Henri Etienne seemed destined for the job of running the world's most iconic art museum. Born into money and minor nobility, he had been educated in art history at the Sorbonne. Extensively traveled, he had held various government cultural posts and spent time running the Cluny, Paris's collection of medieval art, before becoming director of the Louvre at only 52 years old. His file photo showed a lean, handsome man with noble Gallic features. His only listed vices were a mistress (which barely constituted a vice in the eyes of the French police and was only included for the sake of completeness), the occasional overindulgence in wine that had never affected his work, and a twice-annual trip to Monaco where he usually lost in the low five figures. The report noted that his personal fortune could absorb his bad luck at the baccarat table and he was not in any financial difficulty.

Nice life. Jacob felt like slapping him.

Henri Etienne was also a hard worker and a man of meticulous habits. He left his office at eight o'clock sharp every night and walked the four blocks to his home, stopping at an exclusive brasserie for a light dinner and a carafe of fine wine. The report noted that he had not changed his habits and had refused a police escort, saying that the neighborhood was safe and he had not been a target of the thieves, both of which were true.

Jacob parked illegally near the brasserie—one of the perks of working for the CIA is that you never had to pay your parking tickets—and they got out.

Looking around to assess the situation as he always did, he noted CCTV cameras at the nearby intersection, and a gendarme posted in front of a bank a block away. The streets were quiet except for a few pedestrians and the occasional car. This was mostly a business neighborhood and the brasserie and another restaurant a few doors down were the only places on this block that were open.

For some reason, this peaceful Parisian evening made him feel exposed. Perhaps it was because all he had was a 9mm automatic hidden in his jacket, courtesy of a CIA contact who had met them at Charles de Gaulle airport. Jana was similarly armed. He told himself he didn't need heavy weaponry to deal with some blue-blooded art expert, but still, the hairs prickled on the back of his neck.

He slowed, then stopped. The brasserie was only a few yards away; light coming out of its glass door cast a warm golden pool on the sidewalk.

"What is it?" Jana asked, her voice hushed.

"I'm not sure."

He stared at the pool of light. It was changing color, turning darker.

A sudden babble of voices inside. The door burst open and several prosperous looking men and women hurried out, a haze of smoke following them. They were followed by a young waiter, who tried to calm them and sounded apologetic.

*Why isn't the smoke alarm going off?*

*Because someone disabled it, I'll bet.*

Instinctively, Jacob reached into his jacket to hold the butt of his gun, although he didn't draw it. He walked forward, Jana at his side.

The door burst open again, and Henri Etienne and another waiter came out, carrying an old lady between them. She could barely walk and her frail body heaved and shuddered with coughs.

Etienne gave a fearful look inside, then noticed Jacob and Jana approaching.

His eyes went wide and he took off running, the old woman nearly falling as he let go of her.

Jacob cursed, suddenly seeing the situation through Etienne's eyes. A mysterious fire, the alarm doesn't go off, he comes outside, and two strangers are approaching him, both with their hands inside their jackets.

After the thefts, murders, and terror attacks, Etienne had jumped to the obvious conclusion.

The wrong one, but still the obvious one.

Jana shouted something in French, but the museum director ignored her and picked up speed, pelting down the road.

They pursued, leaving the curious crowd to stare. Jacob wondered what the gendarme back at the bank was doing but figured he wouldn't get to the scene in time to make any difference, not with how fast

Etienne was trying to make a getaway. For an art historian, this guy sure could run.

Etienne took a right down a side street and Jacob followed with Jana right behind him. Jacob took the corner at full speed, hoping his quarry hadn't doubled back in order to spring a surprise. Etienne looked too scared for that and nothing in his dossier indicated he had training in anything more combative than hunting wildfowl.

Rounding the corner, he saw the street deserted; besides a few doorways, the only place he could have gone was another side street close by on the left.

*You're not as clever as you think you are.*

Jacob and Jana sprinted down the street, glancing at each doorway as they passed. Except for a portly man coming out of a building with a little poodle on a leash, they saw no one.

He and Jana rounded the next corner and saw Henri Etienne running for all he was worth down the lane, heading for a little square beyond.

Again Jana shouted something in French. The museum director glanced over his shoulder but kept on running.

Jacob picked up speed and began to gain on him.

He almost had him when Etienne made it to the little square. A bronze statue of a man riding a dolphin spouted water into a marble basin. Tidy flowerbeds looked black in the night. Three other lanes exited from the square, but he wouldn't reach any of them. Jacob was almost upon him.

A shot rang out. Jacob glimpsed the muzzle flare from a rooftop to the right. Henri Etienne stumbled, as if he had tripped on a cobblestone, and fell to his knees, clutching his stomach.

Jacob stopped, whipping out his pistol.

Another shot. Etienne jerked and fell hard on the cobblestones.

# CHAPTER THIRTEEN

Jacob dove for cover, tucking into a roll and ending up behind the bronze statue and its marble basin.

Just in time. A bullet panged off the nude bronze man riding a dolphin.

Jacob crawled to one side of the basin and dared a peek. He got rewarded with another shot cracking off the cobblestone inches from his head.

*Sniper's rifle. No IR sight or I'd be dead already.*

Jacob fired three quick shots, more to get the guy's head down than with any hope he'd hit. With a pistol and poor lighting at this range, hitting anything would be more luck than skill.

Jacob ducked back out of sight before the guy could answer.

This had obviously been planned. There must have been a second assassin who had literally smoked him out of the restaurant to lead him to this sniper hidden up here, knowing he'd come this way. It was his way home, after all.

So why not just wait until he came out of the restaurant? They must have been in a hurry for some reason.

Maybe they knew the CIA had sent someone to question him.

How could they know that? A leak?

All this flashed through Jacob's mind in an instant. Now it was time to get back to work.

"You all right?" he called back to Jana, who had run for cover around the nearest building at the entrance to the street where they had chased Henri Etienne.

"Yeah!"

"Cover me."

He glanced again at the rooftop and saw a shadow move.

Jana fired. Jacob burst out of cover and zigzagged through the square toward the building, firing as he went. Lights had come on in several windows, and a couple of foolish civilians, not being able to tell a gunshot from any other loud noise, had actually come out onto their balconies.

The sniper didn't fire back. Jacob didn't flatter himself into thinking that it was his and Jana's pistol fire that cowed him. No, he was retreating.

They couldn't let him get away. They needed clues to this mystery and it looked like the bastard had taken out the one man who could have given it to them.

Jacob got to the building from which the man had fired. It had an ornate façade of stone balconies, columns, and nude women holding up the cornice and balconies.

He holstered his pistol, leapt up, and grabbed the first naked lady he could, one hand grabbing her head and the other grabbing … something else.

*Very firm,* Jacob thought. *A bit cold, though.*

He hauled himself up, vaulted onto the balcony, ignored a scream he heard on the other side of the window, and stood on the railing.

The stone woman holding up the next balcony was just out of reach, but an ornate bronze plaque with the year "1908," advertising the date of the building, was several inches lower.

He leapt for it, hoping it was bolted into the wall securely enough to hold his weight.

As his fingers grasped it, it creaked, shifted, and held.

His feet had nothing to brace against, so he smeared them against the wall to add a bit of friction and did a pull-up, just enough to be able to grab an ornate floral arrangement of stone below the woman. He lifted himself up, got onto the next balcony, and stood on the railing. A shot rang out, sounding like a 9mm. Jacob didn't have time to look.

Luckily this next level had a horizonal stone floral frieze nicely within reach. Jacob had always thought turn-of-the-century buildings were overly decorated. Now he was grateful for that.

Up to another level, and standing on another person's balcony railing. A middle-aged couple, drinks still in hand, stared at him from the other side of the glass but didn't dare interfere. He flashed them a grin and a wave and leapt up to a winged woman who seemed to be holding up the cornice. From there it was simply a matter of a pull-up and trusting an iron drain would hold his weight.

It did, with only a bit of groaning and shaking in protest. Good, old-fashioned craftsmanship. If he had tried that with a modern aluminum drain he would have brought down the whole thing.

Now came the tricky part. He had to pull himself up and get onto the tiles of the sloping roof, making himself a perfect target. Hopefully that guy hadn't stuck around.

He lifted himself up, scrambled on the tile until he got purchase, and got his entire body onto the roof.

No shots came. The assassin had bolted.

He allowed a moment to simply lie there, panting, and grateful that he had just won an epic battle against gravity and common sense.

He scanned the top of the roof. No one.

"He went to the right!" Jana called out. "I've tried to stop the bleeding but Etienne needs a doctor fast. I'll pursue on the street."

*Wimp,* Jacob thought with a smile. *But smarter than me.*

He scrambled up to the roof ridge just in time to see a dark figure moving along the far end of the next building. Jacob ran after him, balancing on the top of the gabled roof.

The assassin, wearing a black balaclava and matching shirt and pants, made it to the edge of the building. Dead end. A lane separated the building from the next one, and it was too far to jump.

The assassin ran down the back side of the gabled roof and Jacob saw his destination; only a narrow garden separated the building they were on from the one behind. Jacob turned and ran down the roof too.

Crazy. They were three stories up, and running down a sloped roof, getting more and more momentum. Downward momentum.

At the last moment, just before plunging off the end of the roof to shatter his bones below, Jacob leapt as high as he could upwards.

His forward momentum made him sail across the narrow garden, where he caught a glimpse of a statue of Cupid, bow and arrow raised high, ready to impale him if he fell.

He hoped that leap up in the air would give him enough upward momentum to negate the downward momentum he had developed.

It did. Partially. His feet landed right on the edge of the opposite roof, but by then he was going more downward than forward and he wavered there for a heart-stopping second, arms cartwheeling, feeling himself falling backwards as the iron grip of gravity pulled him toward his fate.

Jacob did the only thing he could do—yank out his feet from underneath him, kicking backwards.

So instead of toppling off the ledge like a felled tree, he did a faceplant on the rooftiles.

He felt a burst of pain and saw a flash of light. He might have blanked out for a half second.

What woke him up was his slow slide off the roof.

He clawed at the tiles, tried to get enough friction with his palms, but nothing worked.

Jacob kept sliding off the roof.

And then, a minor miracle. His fingertips caught a gap left by a chip in one of the tiles, a little divot that he could press two fingers into with all his might, giving him just enough of a grip to stop his slide off the edge.

His other hand groped around, found another chipped section, and with the hold in both of these, managed to haul himself up enough to swing a knee onto the edge.

From there it was easy enough to clamber up onto the roof.

Just in time for a bullet to buzz over his head.

The assassin had fired at him from the other end of the building with a pistol.

A pistol? Yes, he carried a bag slung across his shoulder. He must have disassembled his sniper's rifle to make an easier and more discreet getaway.

Lucky for Jacob. But while his first shot went wild, the guy's next shot would hit. He was bracing his arm and taking aim. Jacob rolled to the left, knowing that wouldn't be enough.

A shot. A brief moment of surprise that he was still alive.

The assassin ducked down. That hadn't been him firing, but Jana!

She was down in the street somewhere. Jacob didn't have time to look. He pulled out his pistol and saw the assassin had disappeared down the other side of the gabled roof.

Jacob approached the roof ridge in a low crawl, angling right a little to reduce the range between himself and his quarry and make the spot he would appear unpredictable.

Not unpredictable enough. As he poked his head over the roof ridge, a bullet cracked a tile inches away.

The assassin was on the far end of the building, lying prone so Jana couldn't shoot at him.

Right beside him was empty air for a few feet before the next building, an alley that he could easily jump.

But not while Jacob could fire at him and Jana was smart enough to position herself to shoot him right out of the air if he tried to make the jump.

"You're trapped!" Jacob shouted in Arabic. To emphasize his point, a police siren wailed in the distance. "Give yourself up."

"Die, pig!" the man shouted back in Arabic.

Arabic with an Egyptian accent.

He fired again, but Jacob ducked down in time.

"Jana! Cover him. He's right on the edge and wants to jump across the alley."

"I'm on it!"

Jacob smiled. *Of course you are.*

He edged further to the right and popped up just in time to see the assassin turn to aim down at Jana.

Jacob fired and the assassin jerked, then spun around. Only a graze and he was still in the fight.

He fired a shot at Jacob that went wide, then ran for the edge. He was going to dare a jump while under fire.

Jacob shot him in the leg.

The assassin stumbled and tipped over the side.

*Damn it!*

At the last instant, the assassin managed to grab the lip of the roof. Jacob hurried over.

He was still clinging to the roof edge when Jacob made it to him.

Jacob braced himself and reached out a hand.

"I'll pull you up."

The police siren wailed louder.

The assassin looked him in the eyes.

"Why go to prison when I can go to paradise?"

He let go. Jacob stared, horrified, as the assassin turned his body in the air so that he'd land head first on the cobblestones, snapping his neck and dying instantly.

***

Jana saw the whole terrible thing. The man had embraced death rather than be saved by an infidel.

She'd seen this before and it always made her feel ill. How could anyone turn a religion into such death worship?

But there was someone else, someone alive, who needed her help. She sprinted back to the plaza where Henri Etienne lay bleeding onto the cobblestones. She'd had time only to give him a handkerchief to press against the worst of his wounds. No one else had come out to help him, fearful of the gunfight.

Someone had called the police, though. That siren was almost at the scene.

She rushed to Etienne's side. The first shot had pierced his midsection and bled badly. Jana suspected internal bleeding. The handkerchief she'd given him was completely soaked. The second got him in the arm, the same arm that just minutes ago he had used to support an old woman overcome with smoke inhalation.

Jana pulled out a second handkerchief and applied pressure to the wound in his midsection, knowing it would not be enough.

"Monsieur Etienne, can you hear me?"

The museum director tried to focus his eyes on her.

"Who are you?"

"I'm Jana Peters, an archaeologist. I'm trying to find the people who stole the Staff of Ra."

"Someone … chased me."

"We weren't chasing you. We were trying to save you. We killed the man who shot you."

Henri Etienne let out a sigh. He was fading fast.

"Do you have any idea who stole the Staff of Ra, or what they're searching for? Or where they're going to hit next?"

She realized she was getting desperate. The poor man probably couldn't even make sense of what she was saying.

His eyes began to shut.

"Monsieur Etienne? Monsieur Etienne!"

His eyelids fluttered open again, although his eyes remained unfocused.

"They didn't steal … the staff."

"What?"

"They didn't … "

"Is it still hidden in the Louvre?"

Etienne shook his head slowly and began to fade.

"They only got … an inscription."

# CHAPTER FOURTEEN

Les Frères Michaux were, as their name hinted, two brothers. They shared a spacious apartment on the top floor of an exclusive building in downtown Paris, the kind of turn-of-the-century place that Jacob now knew he could climb if he needed to.

This time he didn't need to. A gendarme met them at the door along with the building's porter, an older gentleman who looked like he had just been roused from his sleep and wasn't too happy about it. A quick call to Tyler Wallace had gotten Jacob a contact in the Paris police who had brought him and Jana here.

They went up an old-style wooden elevator encased in an ornate ironwork cage past marble staircases to the top floor, where the gendarme rang the bell. It was answered by a refined-looking gentleman in a silk dressing gown who the gendarme greeted as Monsieur Michaux. He looked to be in his thirties, far too young to have amassed such a fortune except either by inheritance or dishonesty or both. After a few words in French, the gentleman turned to Jacob and Jana and switched to English.

"This is highly irregular, but considering the circumstances please do come in. Are you sure Monsieur Etienne is dead? What a tragedy! I was only speaking with him last week."

"About what?" Jacob asked as they passed through a marble front hall adorned with marble busts of Roman emperors. Jacob didn't know if they were genuine but he had a pretty good idea they were. Another gentleman, the identical twin of the first and wearing a matching dressing gown, appeared from a side door. After another brief explanation, they went to a sumptuous living room adorned with bronze statuettes of Greek athletes and a few Impressionist paintings. The lights of Paris twinkled outside floor-to-ceiling windows. They sat on uncomfortable gilt chairs.

"I'm Jacob Snow with Interpol and the CIA, and this is my partner Jana Peters, an archaeologist by training," Jacob said, failing to mention that his Interpol ID was a forgery and Jana was not officially his partner. The statement had the desired effect, though. Both twins looked identically nervous.

"We will help in any way we can. Does this have something to do with the attack in Egypt?"

"You sold a number of items to Frederick Caldwell of the British Museum, either directly or via Eastern Antiquities in London."

"We have."

"He's dead."

"What?" both antiquities dealer said in unison.

"Killed no doubt by the same people who killed Alphonse Chaput and Henri Etienne. We have reason to believe that the group behind the terror attack at Giza has been killing museum curators and art collectors. You might be next and I'm willing to offer you police protection."

The gendarme, who had been chosen for his good English, turned out to have a good poker face too. There had been no discussion of police protection. That was the carrot. Now Jacob offered the stick.

"We have reason to believe you have been selling illegal antiquities, specifically some Egyptian antiquities. The French police aren't in the habit of offering protection to lawbreakers."

The twins sputtered for a moment and then composed themselves.

"We'll do whatever we can to assist the authorities."

"Damn right you will. So what did you sell to Caldwell?"

"Nothing directly. You're correct that we sold some items via Eastern Antiquities. It's easier for an established dealer to import larger items than a private individual."

"So what did you sell him?"

"Two large friezes from the Sudan."

"Can we see the records for them?"

"Caldwell requested that they be destroyed. He was a very private man and didn't want to be bothered by other collectors."

"Did you destroy them?"

"We destroyed the photographs and the initial translation, but kept the records for the purchase from a dealer in Khartoum and his initial description. We have to keep such documents. It's the law."

Jana cut in. "We need the name and contact information for this dealer, and we'd like to see the records he gave you."

One of the twins went to the next room, the gendarme in tow, and returned with a file folder. Opening it up, they saw a few pages of government applications and export permissions in Arabic, plus the corresponding paperwork on the French side. The letterhead said, "Omar al-Tayib, Genuine Antiquities" with an address in Khartoum.

83

The description of the two pieces included the dimensions, weight, and a summary.

"Item One: Panel showing Pharaoh Senusret III making offerings to Statue of Ra holding staff while his general, Sekhmet, and Anubis look on. Partial inscription reads, 'The great king asks Ra to unleash his power to smite the Nubians in the fifth year of his reign. The ... '

"Item Two: Hieroglyphic frieze of Hymn to Ra plus invocation of the Staff of Ra at the House of Fire."

"What's the House of Fire? I've never heard that reference before," Jana asked.

"That's unclear," one of the twins replied. "It's not been found in any other inscription we're aware of. It's one of the unique details that makes this inscription valuable."

"I notice there're no provenance except 'private collector.'"

"Yes. You'd have to ask the man in Khartoum for details."

"There's a civil war in the Sudan right now."

"You might still be able to get in contact via email or phone. The country isn't entirely cut off."

Jana's brow furrowed as she studied the descriptions.

"It's odd that the offering is to the Statue of Ra and not Ra. The ancient Egyptians thought of the statues of the deities to be living embodiments of the divine."

"Yes, it is a strange phrasing, as is the presence of the general. Usually all the figures in such a representation are all divine, including the pharaoh of course."

*That ties in with my theory of the Staff of Ra being a weapon to attack the Nubians,* Jacob thought.

Jacob leaned forward. "Did you sell Eastern Antiquities any other items that Caldwell ended up buying?"

"They only acted as import agent for these two items, but they did purchase a number of Egyptian and Nubian artifacts from us. Caldwell might have purchased some."

Jacob thought for a moment. "Did you sell Eastern Antiquities any small items from Nubia, anything that had to do with Ra?"

"Small items? Why yes, there was a tiny figurine of Ra from Nubia."

"Did it carry a staff?"

"Yes."

"And did Caldwell buy that?"

"I don't know."

84

"And where did you buy it from?"

"A wholesaler in Marseilles that specializes in bulk sales of antiquities of lesser value."

"Mediterranean Heritage?"

The twins exchanged a look. "Why, yes. You've heard of it?"

"Yeah, I've heard of it."

And it confirmed where he needed to go next--Tunisia. He had a contact in Sfax, a Mediterranean port in the North African country, who was one of their major suppliers.

***

Tyler Wallace was in the French government war room, acting as liaison for the United States. An hour before, they had received news that the Louvre director had been assassinated and that Jacob and Jana were on the scene. They'd also gotten the strange report that Etienne's last words were that they hadn't stolen the Staff of Ra but only an inscription, something that made no sense to anybody, and it turned out that the director was the last person alive who had known what was in the case they had stolen.

To say the French were outraged would be like saying tourism in Egypt was experiencing a slight downturn.

Monsieur Dubois stormed around the war room, shaking his fists and shouting, "It's unacceptable. Unacceptable!" to anyone who would listen, which turned out to be no one. The French generals and the Paris chief of police didn't seem to have much respect for him.

They did agree that the two CIA agents should have done more. Tyler was getting a lot of nasty looks and mumbled comments in French. While he didn't speak the language, it didn't take a genius to figure out what they were saying.

But people were being practical too. While one general was on the phone to the president about the possibility of paying the ransom, a possibility that still seemed remote, other officers and intelligence operatives from several European nations put their heads together to try and figure out what the group's next target would be. Others monitored raids by four different nations' special forces on six different terrorist bases.

Tyler Wallace didn't think any of those raids would hit the right terror cell. They'd been launched out of desperation on the slimmest of evidence.

Tyler's phone rang. Jacob.

"We need a plane to Sfax, sir. I know a man there. He's got deep connections in the Egyptian criminal underworld."

"I know who you mean," Tyler said, looking around at his hostile colleagues and not wanting to say the name out loud. "Why do you think he'd be of help?"

"Because he supplies Mediterranean Heritage with Egyptian and Sudanese antiquities, including a statue of Ra with a staff purchased by Caldwell, one of the items that appears to have been stolen. I'm thinking that since he's one of the biggest suppliers of illegal antiquities from those two countries, our terrorist friends have probably been in touch."

"You've convinced me," Tyler said. He looked around the war room and spotted the representative from MI6 consulting some satellite images and speaking with a French colleague. "I'll get you a British private jet."

"Why not a French one?"

"They're not happy with your progress."

"What do they expect, that we solve this in an hour? They're the ones who failed to protect him. If we hadn't come along, the shooter would have gotten away along with whoever set that fire."

They still hadn't caught the arsonist.

"I know, I know. But the fewer favors we ask of the French right now, the better."

"All right."

"Be ready to leave within an hour, Agent Snow. Time is of the essence."

\*\*\*

Jacob snapped awake as the private jet hit the tarmac at Sfax–Thyna International Airport. He looked at his watch. Less than 24 hours to go, and no word from Tyler Wallace. That meant the ransom hadn't been paid, the raids had hit the wrong terror cells and uncovered no information, and no one had come up with any reliable intel on the group's next target, or even confirmation that it really was The Sword of the Righteous they were dealing with.

And it wasn't like they were the only agents on the ground. The U.S., Canada, and every European nation had sent out every available operative to hunt these people down. The Egyptians had packed

86

thousands of suspects into the prisons. Still no one had come up with any solid leads. How the hell could he and Jana be expected to do any better?

Jana stirred next to him. She had fallen asleep with her head on his shoulder, a rare, pleasant moment in this shitstorm.

She yawned, looked out the window at the Tunisian night, and stretched.

"Get enough sleep?" she asked.

"No, and you?"

"Do I ever when this stuff happens?"

They both laughed. The jet taxied to the gate and they gathered their things.

"So where are we going?" Jana asked.

Jacob smiled. "Well, since our vacation in Delos got cut short, I decided to take you to the beach."

# CHAPTER FIFTEEN

The inflatable motorboat barely stayed above water as its antiquated engine coughed and puttered, pushing the vessel out to sea. It was dark, and all Jacob could see of the passengers was a few lights from their phones.

That showed him enough. They were packed on board, way more than the boat's safe carrying capacity, and probably supplied with barely any drinking water and only what food they had themselves brought along.

While Jacob and Jana, hunkered behind a sand dune facing the beach, couldn't see their faces, they knew where they were from— Pakistan and Afghanistan, Iraq and Syria, a multitude of countries in sub-Saharan Africa. All hoping to get refugee status in the European Union.

They might get it. More likely, they'd end up in a detention center waiting for months for their case to be heard, or they might get detained by the Tunisian Coast Guard and end up back where they started. Those were the lucky options. Many ended up at the bottom of the sea.

A flicker of light on the beach showed Jacob his quarry. A portly man said something in Arabic to two burly companions. Jacob couldn't catch the words. The three men, seen only as shadows against the moonlit surf, turned and started walking toward the dune.

Jacob and Jana waited, each gripping a Heckler and Koch G3 assault rifle, courtesy of the SAS. It was one the UK's Special Air Service's favored weapons and had been part of a gift from their British pilot.

Just as the three men started up the steep seaside slope of the dune, Jacob and Jana rose.

"Freeze!" Jacob said. "Don't try anything, Skander."

Skander Khemiri ran this people smuggling operation, and he was not only a scumbag, but also a coward. He threw his hands up so quick Jacob was surprised they didn't rip from their wrists and go flying up to the moon.

His two companions were made of sterner stuff, and hesitated.

"We got you in our sights. Draw those guns and we'll shoot you down," Jacob snarled.

All three men froze. Jacob sauntered over while Jana shifted to the right to cover him.

Patting them down, he retrieved compact automatics from the two guards but nothing from their boss. Skander Khemiri didn't have the guts for a gunfight. The way he was trembling, he'd have probably shot off his own toe.

"Where are my other two men?" the people smuggler asked.

"Still at their posts. Sleeping. Now you two mugs can walk down to the waterline and stay there. Your boss and I are going to have a chat."

They looked at Skander, who nodded. The pair backed off and went down to the water. Out to sea, the lights of the motorboat had dimmed in the distance, the puttering engine sounding weak.

Jana walked down to Jacob's side.

"This is your informant?" she asked with obvious disgust.

"Yeah. Not exactly a model citizen, but no man who is willing to talk to us is better connected to the Egyptian underworld."

"He's not on the payroll, is he?"

"No. He's simply allowed to exist."

Jana muttered something under her breath. Jacob suddenly felt embarrassed, as he always did when she witnessed the dirtier side of international espionage.

Skander Khemiri glanced over his shoulder to make sure his guards were out of earshot and asked, "How can I help you, my friend?"

"The Giza attack, obviously."

"Of course. I have heard it was The Sword of the Righteous. I heard they were behind the Louvre robbery as well."

"How trustworthy are your sources?" Jana asked.

Skander laughed. "Trustworthy? You may speak good Arabic, madam, but your choice of words is faulty. None of my friends are trustworthy. Well-informed, yes, but never trustworthy."

"What do you know of the Staff of Ra?" Jana asked.

Skander cocked his head. "That's not a legend?"

"Just answer the question."

"It is said that a French archaeological team discovered it near Karnak a century ago, a gold inscribed staff that could shoot radiation, except age meant it leaked. It was hidden in the Louvre because it killed many members of the excavation team. Was that what they were after? It's real?"

"Inscribed?" Jacob asked. "You said it was inscribed."

"Yes. I don't know the details, but the inscription was a devotional text to the statue of Ra. I don't know any more. I'm not an archaeologist; I'm a businessman."

The statue of Ra again. But Jana said the ancients believed the gods and their representations were one and the same. They wouldn't differentiate like that.

"A hell of a business you got here," Jana growled.

Skander glanced over his shoulder. "Don't judge me. I provide hope to the poor."

"By taking all their money and launching them on deathtraps."

"Each passenger gets a life jacket, a real one. Not stuffed with Styrofoam like other smugglers give them."

Jacob snorted. "Yes, you want them to float, because when they get to the other side, your agents in Europe take the life jackets and retrieve what's inside."

"What's inside?" Jana asked.

The people smuggler turned to her. "Are you CIA?"

"We're asking the questions, Skander," Jacob snapped.

"Ancient artifacts. Small things like scarabs or figurines. We cut out a space in the flotation material of the life jacket and put them inside. Not more than one or two per life jacket. They still float!"

"Only because if a boat goes down, you want to be able to fish out the bodies for the treasure they didn't know they were carrying," Jacob growled. He turned to Jana. "His cousin in Marseilles owns Mediterranean Heritage."

"Now it makes sense," Jana replied. "Was there a bronze figurine recently, one of Ra holding a staff? It came from the Sudan."

"Yes ... there was such a figurine."

"And who was your source for that?" Jacob asked.

"You know I can't—"

Jacob placed the muzzle of his assault rifle between Skander's eyes.

"Omar al-Tayib!"

*The same man who exported the two Nubian slabs that ended up in Caldwell's collection.*

"But he fakes his paperwork to export things via the normal channels," Jacob said.

"Only for the big items. The small ones he sends through me, as do other suppliers. No import fees and no trouble faking the paperwork."

"You been approached by The Sword of the Righteous lately?"

90

Even in the moonlight, he could see the people smuggler go pale.

"Oh, god. You know I can't talk about that. They'll peel my skin off before they douse me with gasoline and set me ablaze!"

Jacob pressed the muzzle of his assault rifle harder against Skander's forehead.

"Not if I perforate your skull first. What did they ask?"

"They wanted to know about the Staff of Ra. This was months ago, long before the Louvre attack. I told them the rumors, but they knew all about those. Then they asked me if I had any objects related to it. I didn't. They put in a standing order. If anything related to it came through, I was to tell them. They'd pay handsomely."

"Did anything come through?"

"No. Just some representations of Ra. Those are common, though."

"Even ones carrying a staff?"

"Sure. It's a common emblem for all the Egyptian gods. The figurine you asked about was sent way before they came to me, otherwise I would have sold it to them. You don't fool around with those people."

Jacob paused, thinking. What didn't make sense was the group busting into the Louvre to steal a small amount of U-235. The place was well-guarded, in the center of a busy city; the heist launched a massive manhunt and only yielded enough radioactive material for a dirty bomb, not a nuke.

It would have been easier to bust into a radiology lab or university nuclear engineering department.

Then there was the ransom and the attack on Giza. That seemed like too much of an attention-getter, like they wanted to distract the authorities from some greater purpose, some true goal.

Etienne's final words to Jana came back to him.

*"They didn't steal the Staff of Ra, only an inscription."*

Before Jacob or Jana could think of any more questions, Skander offered some information without being asked, something he had never done in all of Jacob's dealings with him.

"The man behind it all is an Egyptologist, someone who used to be all science and secularism. Now he's become a radical and wants to destroy it all. And yet from what I hear he wants to use the technology of the ancients to bring jihad to the world. He's learned about a lot of things mainstream science laughed at, like the Staff of Ra. He's also learned things that science doesn't even know about. I'm not sure what. There's only been rumors. He's dangerous, though. He's not your usual terrorist who has a death wish and wants to take down as many people as he can. Those fools are like the mass shooters in your own country, but with religion attached. No, this man is highly intelligent, and while he doesn't mind dying for Allah, he'd rather kill for Allah and live to kill another day. Be careful of him, my friend. He knows more than most, and his knowledge and his knack for survival means that he very well might be in charge of The Sword of the Righteous by now. This is bad for everyone. You think my business will survive under a new Caliphate? No. He will kill me almost as quickly as he kills you, and in a worse way because I trade in pagan artifacts. He must be stopped, my friend, because he makes The Sword of the Righteous something far more than a simple band of terrorists."

*** 

Dr. Moswen Farag studied the photos of the Staff of Ra. One of his more avid followers, yearning for martyrdom, had entered the sealed chamber they had prepared in the safehouse, opened the lead case, and taken photos of the hieroglyphs running along the length of the gold shaft. He had then quickly returned the staff to its lead case.

Emerging from the sealed chamber, he kept clear of the others. While he had removed all metal from his person except for the phone, no one wanted to get close to him. They wanted to fight another day. The soon-to-be martyr sent the images to Dr. Farag.

"What will you do now?" they called over to him as he stood on the other side of the field outside the building.

"I will take a gun and kill some police in the next city," he had called back.

"May Allah guide your hand."

That was the last they had seen of him. While the radiation wouldn't kill him for a couple of months, he wanted to die in battle, a fitting end for one of God's warriors.

And the government of Chad, with its close relations to Russia, one of the great devils of the Western world, deserved to lose some of its police.

Dr. Farag didn't worry about it raising any suspicions. The man would travel as far as he could, and there had been many warriors making revenge killings in the country after the unbelievers had wiped out a cell of the Eternal Jihad a couple of days before.

But no matter how many sellouts to the unbelievers he managed to kill, it would not be even close to the same level of service he had performed by taking those photographs.

The images were speckled with white dots, a product of the radiation, but he had taken enough of them that Dr. Farag could make out the inscription. Slowly, taking care to get every nuance of meaning, he translated the hieroglyphs.

When he discovered their meaning, he raised his hands heavenward and gave thanks.

It was all he had hoped for, and all the unbelievers feared.

They didn't have far to go, and there was no serious opposition to stop them. And when they got there, The Sword of the Righteous would become as powerful as Russia or the United States.

# CHAPTER SIXTEEN

"We have to talk to this Omar al-Tayib in Khartoum," Jana said as they made their way back to the Sfax airport. She cast a nervous glance at the rising sun and felt a tremor of fear. They had less than twelve hours until the deadline. "He's our only potential link to the thieves who took the Staff of Ra."

"We'll go see him."

"In Khartoum? Are you crazy? There's a civil war on there now."

"What's wrong with a little civil war? I've hung out in lots of places with civil wars. You get used to it."

"We'll stick out like sore thumbs. Everyone will see we're foreigners and there aren't any foreigners there right now."

"That's where you're wrong. Both sides have hired Eastern European mercenaries. How's your Russian?"

"Nonexistent."

"Romanian? Serbian?"

"Ditto."

"Then let me do the talking."

She stopped and turned to him. "Do Eastern European mercenary companies ever hire women?"

"Sure! Um … no. Don't worry, we'll think of something. Ah, I know! We'll trade on your archaeological expertise. Tell them you're there to help whatever faction we join to mine for antiquities to trade on the black market for weapons."

"Are you serious?"

Jacob shrugged. "It worked for ISIS."

It was true. While the Islamic State hated all traces of the past and destroyed many ancient buildings in their territory, they also sold smaller artifacts on the black market to get much-needed hard currency for weapons.

"I don't want to live in this world anymore," Jana grumbled.

"Odd attitude for someone trying to save it."

"How are we going to get in? We don't have any paperwork proving we're with any mercenary company."

"The CIA will take care of that. Or MI6. Actually, probably the Brits because we'll have to fly to Egypt first and their people there have better ties to the Sudan. I'll talk with our pilot."

"But what if this is another dead end, or a minor lead that doesn't get us to the bad guys? The clock is ticking and we still have no real idea where they might strike."

Jacob stopped, putting his hands on her shoulders.

"No, we have no real idea what we're doing, and no real idea if we're even getting warmer. That's just how it is sometimes."

"But look at what's at stake!"

Jacob nodded sadly, and Jana felt a tug of pity for him.

"Yeah, it's like that a lot of the time," he said softly. "You do your best with no idea if what you're doing is the right thing or even if you can make a difference. But you do your best because you're the only one in a position to do anything."

*** 

They landed in Khartoum six hours later after a brief stopover in Cairo to pick up documents and switch flights to an MI6 plane registered in Russia. Jana sat next to Jacob and nearby sat three Romanian nationals—Alexandru, Florin, and Radu—who were all naturalized citizens in the United Kingdom. They had all moved to the UK when that country was still in the European Union to look for better lives. After a few unsatisfactory years waiting tables and unclogging drains, all of them had joined the armed forces and ended up in the SAS.

None of them had espionage experience, but they were all seasoned fighters, spoke Russian, Romanian, and English, and had enough tattoos and scars to look like mercenaries.

Jana wished they could have a bigger team along, but the UK, like every other Western democracy, had sent all its available forces on missions against terror cells or onto guard duty at potential targets. These three guys had all been in the same unit and had been slated to go on some raid they couldn't talk about. All of them grumbled about not being with their comrades for the upcoming fight.

"Don't worry," she told them. "You may not be with your buddies, but you'll get plenty of fighting."

Jana, like the others, wore desert camouflage with the emblem of a fake mercenary company sewn onto the arm. She still carried a Heckler and Koch G3 assault rifle, along with a 9mm sidearm, and two shrapnel and two flashbang grenades. The firearms were standard SAS issue. The organization didn't have any spare Russian weapons.

"They've all been sent on a different mission," they'd been told without further elaboration.

Jana shook her head. So much they didn't get to know. Hopefully no one they met in the Sudan would be knowledgeable enough about European weaponry to notice to discrepancy.

Jana suppressed a yawn and checked her watch. Six hours until the deadline and they were landing in a war-torn Third World capital with only the address of a shifty antiquities dealer as a lead. It's amazing the SAS was helping them at all. Jacob, or Tyler Wallace, had a hell of a reputation to draw upon.

As the plane taxied into the private terminal of the almost abandoned airport, Jana looked out the window past the low concrete terminal. In the desert haze she couldn't see much of the city, just a few high-rises and minarets. As the plane turned, she saw a couple of columns of smoke rising in the distance, and realized that much of the haze wasn't from desert dust, but from the capital city burning.

The situation was tough according to the briefing they'd been given via the airplane's radio. There had been no time during their stopover in Egypt to actually have a face-to-face meeting with a local expert.

A few years before, the dictator had been overthrown by the army and a militia called the Rapid Support Forces. Given Africa's long history of military coups, the dictator thought that having two military forces of almost equal size would make them perpetual rivals and secure his place at the top. That worked until it didn't. The two factions united to get rid of him, then ran the show for a while before handing over the reins to a civilian government.

That civilian government didn't last long, and now the Sudanese army and the Rapid Support Forces were slugging it out. The army controlled about two-thirds of the capital and large sections of the countryside, while the Rapid Support Forces controlled the rest.

The fight had been going on for months now, with no side getting the upper hand and thus no end in sight. Neither showed any interest in negotiation.

An MI6 mole in the Sudanese Armed Forces had arranged for their "recruitment" and would meet them at the terminal.

The jet stopped, the gangway came down, and they filed out. The Polish-born UK national who had flown them here gave them a

96

thumb's up. His orders were to stay at the airport to provide them with a quick getaway if they needed it.

They filed out into the searing heat of noonday Sudan. Across the tarmac they saw, standing at the entrance to the terminal, a burly middle-aged man in an officer's uniform and five regular soldiers. Jana and the others marched over to them.

"Do any of you speak English?" the officer asked. Jana hoped this was their mole and that he was just keeping up appearances.

"I do," said Radu, who had the heaviest accent. "We're reporting as scheduled."

"Welcome. I am Major Mohammed Babikir. I hope you had a good flight from Moscow." The privates were staring at Jana. Major Babikir did too. "You didn't mention you had a woman with you."

"An expert in electronic warfare. She'll run the fleet of drones coming on the next flight. She's also an expert on antiquities in case the armed forces need to raise money."

"Excellent. Come with us."

They marched through the terminal, no customs or bag checks needed, and to a waiting Hummer with a driver already at the wheel. The driveway alongside the terminal building was otherwise abandoned. No passenger flights and very few cargo flights made it into Khartoum airport these days.

Major Babikir switched to Arabic and addressed the privates. "You may go back to your regular duties. I'll handle our Russian guests from here."

Once they were gone, he turned to the group and addressed them in English.

"My driver can be trusted. He is my youngest nephew and hates what has happened to our great nation as much as I do. The armed forces is full of brigands and conmen and the Rapid Support Forces are even worse. How can I help you? The only message I got was to expect your arrival."

Jacob stepped forward. "I'm leading this team. We need to go to see Omar al-Tayib, who owns a shop called Genuine Antiquities. Here's the address."

Major Babikir looked at the paper and frowned. "This is very close to the front line."

"Is it in your territory?"

"Yes. He might not be there any longer, though. The area gets shelled sometimes."

"We have to check."

"I can help better if I know what this is about."

Jacob paused. Jana could tell he was trying to gauge the major's loyalty. Moles had a bad habit of switching sides.

"An impending terror attack."

"The same group that attacked Giza?"

"Yes."

He made a face as if he had just sucked on a lemon. "Radicals are destroying my religion. There are many in the Rapid Support Forces. I'll do what I can to help."

Jana wasn't sure if he was being honest or not, and realized they'd just have to take his word for it.

They clambered aboard the Hummer, wrapping kaffiyehs around their head and faces to obscure their white skin. Even in a government vehicle, it was best not to attract attention as they drove through the city. The driver and the major sat in front. Jacob sat right behind the major, and Jana didn't need to be told why.

*I hope this guy can be trusted.*

They set out. The airport road was mostly empty, flanked only by warehouses in dusty lots behind barbed wire fences. Soon, however, they got to the edges of the city, where they had to stop at a checkpoint guarded by a dozen men and an armored personnel carrier.

Major Babikir got them through that easily enough and they entered a more built-up area. Dusty roads were flanked by low buildings with shopfronts on the ground floors. Most of these were closed, the steel shutters down and firmly padlocked. Interspersed with the shops stretched the blank walls of private compounds, where the rich and middle class hid from the storm blowing through their country. In a little square in front of a mosque there was a small market, with sacks of grain and piles of fruits and vegetables. None of the piles were big, the shoppers few and hurried. Jana got the impression there wasn't much to buy and not much money to buy it with.

Peeking out the front of the Hummer, she noticed they were driving straight for one of the columns of smoke she'd seen from the airplane.

"What's burning over there?" Jacob asked, when he noticed her looking.

"A gas station in an RSF neighborhood," the major replied. "We hit it with mortar rounds earlier today."

"Who's winning in this sector?" Radu asked.

The major looked back at the Romanian and smiled bitterly. "If you ask my general, we are inflicting a crushing defeat on the RSF. If you ask the RSF, we have already retreated from their neighborhood. If you ask me, the front line won't change by more than a city block or two this year."

They passed through another checkpoint and entered a more prosperous-looking area. The shops were nicer, or at least seemed so. This close to the front line most remained closed. The buildings were newer and there were even a couple of modern-style office buildings of several stories. One of these had been badly pummeled, its glass shattered, one whole floor burned.

"We are almost there," Major Babikir said. "Just around this next corner."

There came the crackle of gunfire.

"How close to the front are we?" Jacob asked.

"Three blocks. The way the streets are arranged we don't have to worry about snipers this far back, but listen for mortar rounds. They can come at any time."

"Park here. We don't want him to see us coming," Jacob said.

The major nodded to the driver and they pulled into a vacant lot. A couple of goats munched on a few tufts of grass. Jana wondered who was watching them until she spotted a little boy dressed in ragged and dirty white robes in a corner of the lot. He squatted beneath a piece of corrugated steel held up by two stacks of bricks and stones, the boy's handmade bomb shelter.

For a moment she wondered why he was still here, but then she saw more evidence that people remained in this neighborhood—a line of laundry between two buildings, a motorbike securely chained to a fence, even a small shop selling food and household supplies that remained open, although dark inside because there was apparently no electricity.

Many residents had nowhere to go, and nowhere in this city was safe anyway.

Jana felt eyes on her from the screened windows.

They walked in formation, Jacob taking point, the major just behind him giving directions, and the rest strung out in single file behind them. They heard more small arms fire, and the distant thud of a mortar firing and a moment later a boom as its round detonated somewhere.

Jana felt exposed. Too many windows, too many rooftops to shoot down at them from.

But there shouldn't be any RSF troops here; the fighting sounded close but was clearly a couple of blocks away, so they should be safe.

That assumption vanished when rifle fire erupted from three different windows at once.

# CHAPTER SEVENTEEN

The shots came simultaneously, an obvious ambush by a group waiting for them.

Jacob dove into the arched doorway of a clothing shop, its steel shutter keeping him from entering the building. When he looked out again just a moment later he saw Radu lying on the dirt, unmoving. The major's nephew lay groaning nearby. The others had bolted for cover.

All except for Major Babikir. He ran for his nephew, grabbed him by the webbing around his uniform and started to drag him to safety as shots cracked off the pavement all around him.

What the hell was going on? Was this an RSF group that had snuck behind army lines, or someone lying in wait for Jacob and his team? If so, how did they know they were coming?

Jacob opened up on the one window he could see, on the opposite side of the street and two buildings down. It sounded like the two Romanians and Jana started firing too, although he couldn't see them from his position.

He also couldn't see if his fire was having any effect. The window remained a black rectangle in contrast to the brilliant sun outside, the perfect place for a sniper. There was a brief muzzle flare, then again, and then nothing. Jacob had no idea if that meant he had hit the guy or if the shooter was just staying behind cover, waiting for his chance.

At least the major got his nephew to safety.

"The bastards!" he heard the major shout. "I'll kill them all!"

"Is it Sudanese army?" Jana called out from somewhere else. He hoped she'd found some decent cover.

"I don't know," Major Babikir replied. "Oh my God, he's dying."

More fire erupted from a new window across the street, clanging into the metal shutter behind Jacob. The sniper had shifted to get a better angle on him.

Jacob crouched and fired back.

"We need to get into the shop!" Jacob shouted.

"We need to retreat!" Florin shouted back. "We can't hold this position."

"Forward is the safest way. This mission is essential, and this ambush proves it."

He wasn't sure that was true, but he was too close to pull back now.

With a roar, Major Babikir burst from cover and ran down the street, firing his AK-47 as he went.

Jacob fired at the opposite building to cover him, and then slipped out of the doorway to follow.

Stepping into the street again meant he got it from both sides. Jacob ducked and wove, feeling far too exposed. At least Jana, Florin, and Alexandru provided cover fire.

By the time he got two doors down to Omar al-Tayib's Genuine Antiquities shop, the major had blown the lock off the shutter and hauled it up. The doorway was another arched, inset door, made to provide shade for the shopkeeper to sit outside his shop in comfort and greet passersby, an old tradition in the Middle East. That was in happier times. Now it provided cover from the enemy.

But who the hell was the enemy?

"Do you think these are your guys? And how long before the units here respond?" Jacob asked.

Major Babikir, enraged at the loss of his youngest nephew, didn't respond. He shouldered his way through the wooden doors, which gave way with a crash, and charged into the darkened interior. Jacob had no choice but to follow.

They found themselves in a showroom of shelves and pedestals that would have once held antiquities, now cleared out thanks to the war. Disappointment and worry rose in Jacob. It looked like Omar al-Tayib had evacuated.

But then Jacob spotted a couple of slabs of stone hanging on the wall covered in hieroglyphs and bas-reliefs of gods or pharaohs. They were probably worth a lot, and yet they hadn't been taken away. Too heavy? Not enough time?

The antiquities dealer might just still be here.

Major Babikir rushed through the nearly empty showroom and into a hallway beyond. From there, some stairs led up. The windows, while shuttered, allowed enough light to see. Jacob had to run to keep up with the Sudanese officer.

A man with a Kalashnikov swung around the top of the steps. Major Babikir took him out with a single shot.

Omar al-Tayib? Jacob wondered as the man tumbled down the stairs past him. He wore civilian clothing, but looked too young to own such a big business.

Major Babikir rounded a corner, fired off another shot, and dove into a room.

"Ease up!" Jacob said, knowing it was no good. The man had just seen a family member gunned down.

Jacob ran after him and nearly got knocked over as the major jumped back around a corner, bullets chasing him. A spray from an AK-47 on automatic chewed up the far wall.

"How many?" Jacob asked.

"Just one."

"How far?"

The unseen enemy fired again, keeping them from looking.

"Just on the other side of the room. Five meters. Cover me and I'll rush him."

The major's eyes were ablaze.

Jacob pulled out a grenade. "This is the safer way."

Major Babikir snatched it out of his hand, pulled the pin, and chucked it around the corner. There was a startled shout and a bang. Jacob and the major rushed into the room to find their opponent, another young man in civilian clothing, lying dead on the floor, shredded from half a dozen shrapnel wounds.

Together they cleared the upper level, finding no one else. This floor was obviously the living quarters for Omar al-Tayib and his family, but they appeared to have left. Most of the clothes were missing in the wardrobe; there were no computers, and no jewelry box in the woman's room.

"Damn it, they've evacuated!" Jacob shouted.

"They knew we were coming, though," the major said. "I don't think these are RSF fighters. No uniforms or badges and they don't fight as well as the RSF. They are hired gunmen. Your informant tricked you."

"I'll kill him when I see him again," Jacob snarled.

The sound of footfalls downstairs. Jacob and Major Babikir exchanged a worried glance.

"It's us!" Jana called out.

"You all right?"

"Alexandru got wounded. We killed a sniper and captured the other. The army is coming up the block from both directions. We need the major down here fast!"

"I'll speak to them," Major Babikir said. "And pray to God they weren't in on this. Stay here. If they kill me, run out the back."

Jana came up, her gun jammed in the back of a young Sudanese man in civilian dress. Florin helped Alexandru up the stairs. He had been shot through the hand and it bled freely. Major Babikir eased past them and hurried downstairs.

As Florin sat Alexandru down and pulled out a first aid kit, Jacob went to the window and opened the shutters a crack.

An armored personnel carrier rumbled down the street, the man on top aiming a heavy machine gun from behind a steel shield. A column of men followed, using the vehicle as cover, scanning the rooftops. They looked wary and confused, obviously curious as to why there had been shooting behind their lines and now everyone seemed to have vanished except for Radu lying dead in the street and the major's nephew lying dead in a doorway.

The major called from the shop entrance and then came out, his AK-47 slung across his back and keeping his hands in sight. He approached the armored personnel carrier and a man in a captain's uniform climbed out of the hatch. They stopped and conferred.

"Looks like Major Babikir is working things out," Jacob said. He kept his voice down, just in case.

"This filing cabinet is completely empty!" Jana called from another room. "I can't find any documentation at all."

"Maybe he can tell us something," Alexandru said, giving the prisoner a kick. His hand had been bandaged and he had some life back in him now. "Or maybe we can just blow his damn head off."

Keeping one eye on the conversation outside, Jacob turned to the prisoner, who sat, all fight taken out of him, despondent on the floor.

"Talk. The Sudanese army is outside. Want me to hand you over to them? Or to the army major whose nephew you killed? Who are you and who told you to attack us?"

The man slumped. "I don't know anything."

Another kick from the wounded Romanian got him talking.

"We were hired by a local imam. He said we should hide in these buildings because some infidels were coming to the house of Omar al-Tayib. He paid us well. I lost my job because of the civil war. We all did. And none of us wanted to join the army or the RSF. So we did this."

"Did they say we were coming today? When did the imam hire you?"

"Last night. We had to sneak into position under cover of darkness. He said you were coming today or tomorrow."

*Skander must have narced on us the minute we left. God, I'll kill that guy!*

"Why did the imam want us dead?"

"He was following orders."

"From whom?"

The man's eyes got shifty. Alexandru kicked him again.

"From whom?"

"The Sword of the Righteous. They are not a group you say no to."

"They have a cell here in Khartoum?"

"They have cells everywhere. I have heard one of their leaders came here, an Egyptian professor."

"Professor of what?"

"Archaeology, but he has embraced religion now and cast aside his unbelieving ways."

A gasp from the doorway made them turn.

Jana stood there, staring at the prisoner.

"A professor of archaeology from Egypt?" she asked. "Are you sure?"

"That's what I've heard from people in the mosque. Many have allied themselves with The Sword of the Righteous."

"Which mosque is it?"

The man shook his head. "No. I will give you the names of foreigners in this group, but I will not tell you the name of my mosque or its imam."

Alexandru kicked him again, and Florin gave him a kick too.

"Stop," Jacob said.

"We'll beat the answer out of him!" Alexandru snarled.

"You haven't worked in the Middle East much, have you?" Jacob asked.

"Not at all," Florin said.

"I didn't think so, because if you did, you'd know this guy would rather die than give you that information. The mosque community is like a family. You'd be just as likely to get him to tell you how to kill his brother or son. Not going to happen." Jacob turned to the prisoner. "So you're not in The Sword of the Righteous?"

"No, and neither is my imam. But they give us funds. We needed to repair the building and they gave us money for this. They also gave money for some of those who were jobless, and fixed the water line in the neighborhood."

Jacob nodded. This was a typical tactic of extremist groups in this region. When a poor and corrupt central government failed to provide basic services, a terror group would step in and, with money that usually came from rich donors in the Gulf, would do what the government couldn't or wouldn't do. It was a classic way to buy loyalty, although it sounded like this local imam didn't want to commit to the group fully. On the other hand, he was probably too afraid not to do what he was told.

The sound of heavy boots on the stairs. Major Babikir stomped into the room with several soldiers. They grabbed the prisoner.

"We're taking him in for questioning," the major said.

"Don't kill him," Jacob said. "We might need him for information, and we need you to get us around town."

The major glared at the prisoner, hesitated, and nodded. "This piece of dirt can wait. Where do you need to go?"

"First, we need to get Alexandru back to the plane, and then … "

He wasn't sure what to do then. He looked at Jana, who had been trying to get his attention for the last few moments. She nodded to the doorway.

"One moment. If you take Alexandru down to the Hummer, we'll join you shortly."

The major nodded and the soldiers and SAS men posing as mercenaries moved toward the stairway, the prisoner a sad, slumped form in the middle. Jacob and Jana went to the other room to confer in private.

"What is it?" he whispered.

"I think I know who's behind all this," she replied.

# CHAPTER EIGHTEEN

Jana watched as Jacob looked over his shoulder to see if someone might be listening. Despite having gone through a gunfight together, she could tell he still didn't fully trust the Sudanese armed forces. Probably a good idea.

"So who do you think is behind this?" he asked.

"When that Sudanese gun for hire said there was an Egyptian archaeologist who had radicalized here in the Sudan, it all clicked. Ever since the Suez Canal incident, I've been doing some research into Egyptologists. It's obvious there must have been an expert helping them, someone who could read hieroglyphics and who could have heard about the mysterious power of Ra the ancients had supposedly contained and used. That's very specialized information. I've been an archaeologist all my working life and I'd never heard about this supposed power, and of course I can't read hieroglyphics. That takes a decade at least to study."

"So you were thinking some Egyptologist went rogue. The CIA looked into that and couldn't find anyone."

"That's because you believed his cover story."

"Whose cover story?"

"Dr. Moswen Farag. He retired from Cairo University a few years ago when he was only in his early fifties, after a successful career as an Egyptologist. He claimed he was in poor health, but I found he had attended a large number of academic conferences even after his retirement, especially conferences on ancient technology. He also got invited to Saudi Arabia and Bahrain, supposedly as a historical consultant."

"Rich citizens of both of those countries have been funding The Sword of the Righteous."

"I know. Remember how you shared a dossier on the group with me?"

Jacob smiled. "That top secret dossier I could get fired if not imprisoned for sharing with a civilian? Yeah, don't spread that around too much."

Jana chuckled. "I won't. Now none of this would have been so suspicious except that Dr. Moswen Farag is also a specialist in the Greco-Roman period catacombs in northern Egypt."

"That's where they found the Canopic jar!"

"Exactly."

Jana cringed inwardly. In that terrifying subterranean fight they had with the terrorists, the gunfire had set off a cave-in that had destroyed a large portion of an irreplaceable historic monument.

That kept happening. The damage to the Temple Mount in Jerusalem, the destruction of a preserved pirate ship in South America, and now the Great Pyramid of Giza getting blasted. It seemed like she had switched from being an archaeologist to being a terrorist hunter who ended up causing collateral damage to world heritage.

"So you think this guy is the same expert we've been hearing about?" Jacob asked.

"Yes, because get this. His other specialty is the Egyptian colonization of Nubia. He'd know about the legends of the Staff of Ra. He'd know about the pharaoh Senusret III. It all makes sense. The same man is expert in the same subjects The Sword of the Righteous was involved in for both attacks."

"And this proves The Sword of the Righteous is behind this! We didn't have solid evidence until now. We were just going on the assumption that only one group would know about the naturally occurring U-235."

"So if that's the case, then they might be planning to hit the same target as last time."

Jacob's jaw dropped.

"The Suez Canal," he whispered. "Damn. But why blow up a pyramid and put the Egyptians on high alert?"

"Maybe a couple of reasons. First, it distracts them into thinking their heritage is what's being targeted, and it distracts the world into thinking the same thing. How many of the West's resources have gone into defending places like the Eiffel Tower and the Acropolis? Everyone's stretched so thin as to get to the breaking point."

"Yeah, but ever since the first attack the Egyptians have doubled their protection around the canal."

"Is that still the case? Have they drawn off men to guard the ports and the archaeological sites?"

"Hmm, I see what you mean. They probably have."

"And while the Giza attack is a strike against paganism and the Egyptian government, hitting the Suez Canal with a dirty bomb would disrupt the entire world economy."

Jacob snapped his fingers. "And Sudan isn't a bad place to launch the attack from. Since the civil war, relations with Egypt have deteriorated, plus the government is too divided and distracted by the civil war to monitor their own country. Just look at how we got ambushed two blocks behind the front line! These guys were able to set up and hide for hours. If the terrorists launched from Port Sudan or one of the smaller ports to the north, in a fast boat they could get to the canal in ten hours or less."

"So they might have already left."

"I have to get to my satellite phone back on the plane," Jacob embraced her and planted a kiss on her lips. "You're amazing."

And before she could react, before she could even fully enjoy and return the kiss, he was running out of the building. Jana hurried along behind him, her own feelings taking second place to stopping another bloodbath.

*\*\**

*Two hours later, just south of the southern mouth of the Suez Canal*

Captain George Hudson monitored the speed of the container ship *Windward* from the command deck. It took miles to slow down such a huge vessel, and he had started the deceleration process fifteen minutes ago, though he still couldn't even see his destination, the entrance to the Suez Canal. He checked the GPS and the calculations of his vector toward the entrance and saw he was right on target.

Then he checked his radar, and his brow furrowed. There seemed to be a lot of vessels and airplanes clustered at the entrance to the canal that hadn't been there a few minutes before.

What was going on? Memories of the Suez Canal attack of the previous year came back to him. He'd been on this same route, taking his ship toward the canal, when the terrorists struck. Luckily he was still out in the Indian Ocean, hauling a cargo from Shanghai to Rotterdam, and was able to divert around the Cape of Good Hope. That put him well behind schedule and cost the company tens of thousands of dollars in extra fuel, but the canal had been shut for several days and it couldn't be helped. It hadn't hurt his work record, just the company's bottom line.

Was something similar happening now? There had been that attack on Giza. Had the terrorists struck again?

But he didn't hear any unusual chatter on the marine radio.

He got on the radio, switched to the canal frequency, and called the canal authorities.

"This is the cargo ship *Windward* approaching the canal. Is there an incident occurring? Over."

"Suez Canal authorities to *Windward*. All is fine. Continue at present course and bearing. Over."

"But I see a concentration of small boats and aircraft converging on the southern end of the canal. Over."

"Nothing is amiss. Continue present course and bearing. Over."

He exchanged glances with his first mate.

"What do you think?" Captain Hudson asked.

"I think they're hiding something. Maybe they're conducting a search? Remember how in the Philippines there was that terror threat and they searched all the shipping? They didn't tell us a thing until they were on us."

"Maybe. But what if we were just talking with a terrorist?"

His second in command went pale. "You mean they might have taken over the radio tower?"

"They just blew up a pyramid. Those nutcases are capable of anything!"

The two lapsed into silence. Meanwhile, the *Windward* continued its course toward the Suez Canal, and that confluence of unidentified shipping and aviation.

"We could turn back," the captain said.

"Could we?"

"Chart a course, just in case."

While his first mate got to work, Captain Hudson pulled out a powerful pair of binoculars and scanned the area. Too many captains relied on all the electronic gizmos on board to do their seeing for them. Sometimes it was better to look with your own eyes.

And it didn't take long for his own eyes to notice something wrong.

In front and behind him were other container ships and freighters running in a long line from horizon to horizon, all heading for the canal. On the shore, however, where there was generally nothing but sand and the occasional fishing village, mostly abandoned now that the pollution from one of the world's busiest shipping lanes had poisoned the water, he saw an unprecedented amount of activity. Sunlight gleamed off vehicles and people who, even with the magnification of binoculars, appeared as little dots moving in several locations along the shore.

The Egyptian army? Refugees from some trouble inland? Terrorists?

Captain Hudson got back on the radio.

"*Windward* to Suez Canal control. Could you please inform me of the situation? I'm seeing unusual activity on shore. Over."

"Suez Canal control to *Windward*, maintain current speed and direction. Over."

Captain Hudson turned to his second in command. "Something's wrong."

His first mate didn't look up from his calculations. "Big time. Look, we can turn out of the line and just make a 180 without hitting any other traffic, but we have to decide now."

The captain studied the activity on shore, glanced at the radar showing a gathering cluster of ships and aviation near the mouth of the canal, and hesitated.

Then he remembered the party he had just attended a few days before in Shanghai.

Desh Gupta, the ship's chief electrician, had received a call from his wife in Kerala. She had given birth to a baby girl, their first child. Captain Hudson had taken the whole crew out to a bar celebrate, and Desh had ended up dancing on the table with joy, shouting out that on his next vacation, just a week from now, he would fly from Rotterdam to India and hold his baby girl for the first time.

Desh had to make it back home.

"Turn it around!" Captain Hudson shouted.

His second in command hurried to obey. Together they ran through the coordinates and started to turn the boat to starboard to get it out of the line of tankers.

It took barely a minute before there was a flash of light from the shore to port.

Captain Hudson looked in that direction, but the flash didn't repeat itself.

A second later, a plume of water sprang up not ten meters from their prow.

"Container ship *Windward*, this is Suez Canal security. Return to your previous course immediately or you'll be sunk. Over."

"Jesus Christ! What the hell do you think you're doing?" Captain Hudson shouted into the mic.

Another flash on shore, and another artillery shell spouted up water close by.

"Return to your previous course immediately or you'll be sunk. Over."

"We are! We are!"

He and his first mate hauled the ship back in line.

"Do not vary from your course, *Windward*. Prepare to be boarded. Over."

In the distance, Captain George Hudson saw a line of helicopters flying from shore toward him.

*Looks like Gupta isn't going to get his vacation after all.*

# CHAPTER NINETEEN

"Where to?" the SAS pilot asked.

Jana sat in the back of the jet with Jacob, Alexandru, and Florin just beside them. In the storage hold lay the body of Radu, their comrade. Jacob kept glancing in that direction, his face pained even though the body of their fallen comrade lay out of sight.

They were fully fueled and cleared for takeoff at Khartoum Airport.

For a moment, nobody answered Pavel's question.

"We should get up to the Suez Canal," Jacob said in a quiet voice. "That's where the action is."

He turned to Jana, a silent request for confirmation.

Jana thought a moment. She had no better idea. Now that they knew The Sword of the Righteous really was behind the thefts and attacks, going to Suez made sense. It was the obvious target.

But the group probably assumed that Western intelligence had figured out who they were. So would they risk hitting the same target twice?

Still, she had no better ideas.

"How long to Port Tawfiq?" she asked. That was the port on the southern end of the canal.

"A little less than two hours," the pilot said.

Jana checked her watch. "We have just two hours to deadline."

"I'm painfully aware of that fact," the pilot said.

"Do we have a laptop and Internet access on board?"

"Need to catch up on your email?" the pilot asked.

"Answer the damn question!" the shout came out almost as a shriek. Jana's nerves were too on edge, just as everyone else's.

Pavel stopped looking her in the eye. "Yeah. Florin, hook her up. So where to?"

"The Suez Canal," Jana muttered. "I guess."

The pilot looked to Jacob for approval, which annoyed her even though he was in charge. Jacob nodded.

As the plane taxied down the runway, Florin got her a laptop and she logged into an academic server that gave her access to journal articles and archaeological field reports. There was something she needed to find, and if her hunch was correct, she needed to find it soon.

The plane took off. Jana barely noticed, typing furiously, and scrolling through hundreds of search results.

She wasn't finding it. She kept searching as the plane gained altitude and headed north-northeast, toward Port Tawfiq.

Jana kept searching as it leveled off at a cruising altitude and everyone broke out rations. She didn't even notice when Jacob set some on a tray in front of her.

As the minutes dragged by and the private jet sped toward the Suez Canal, Jana tried to tamp down her frustration. While as an academic she had access to a vast amount of scholarly literature, this actually made her job more difficult. There was just too much to sift through. It didn't help that her specialty was Roman archaeology, not Egyptology and certainly not the study of the Egyptian outposts in Nubia. She was out of her depth.

Yet she continued to swim. She knew there was something here, something to be found. But what?

Then she realized her mistake. She was searching in English. The French had done almost as much work in Egypt and the Sudan, and it had been a French team that had found the Staff of Ra at Karnak.

She switched to French, a language she spoke almost as well as her native English.

It didn't take long to find an excavation report from 1938 of a temple of Ra in northern Sudan.

What she read there changed everything.

While a French team had been excavating an Egyptian border fort dating to the Middle Kingdom, it had come across an extensive temple to Ra buried beneath the sands.

The temple was remarkably preserved, with its walls standing five meters in height. While the crew hadn't had time to remove all the sand that had buried it in the ensuing millennia, they had come across the top of a statue of the sun god.

A statue holding a staff.

An Egyptian border fort. A temple of Ra. A statue of the god holding a staff.

There was even a photo, grainy with age and poor reproduction on the online scan. It showed the head and shoulders of the statue emerging from the sand, and a stone column held in the statue's right

114

hand that was the staff. Atop the staff was a strange, crumpled hunk of metal the crew described as:

"A curious construction of lead, crushed by the weight of the sand that buried it. We chose not to remove it until further investigation next field season."

Jana sat back in her seat, stunned by the possibilities.

It took a minute to collect herself. Vaguely she heard Jacob and the SAS team talking amongst themselves, sounding as if they were in another room even though they sat right next to her. Jana couldn't even focus on what they said.

The article lacked many details, being just a summary of a field season, a common publication to announce big finds while the team worked on the full field report in book form. She dove back into the database, searching for more.

She couldn't find a full field report for excavation. Given that the first field season had been a year before the beginning of World War Two, it was no surprise they never got to publish their findings or go back.

And after the war? No sign that anyone had checked out the site. There were no publications by the lead archaeologist at all.

The only thing that came up on a name search was an obituary.

He had died in 1942, having fled the Nazis to England.

The cause of death? Cancer.

Jana's heart went cold.

She looked up the location of the temple, and found a mention that it was next to the village of Ibn Balamon. A quick search on Google found that to be in northern Sudan, not far from the Egyptian border. She searched for information on the village itself and found it to now be a town, with one of the highest concentrations of Christians in the country.

Christians? More searching told her that Christians made up about one to five percent of Sudan's population, depending on which source she read, compared with about ten percent of Christians in the population of Egypt. No mention of the temple, although there was a brief mention of the fort.

Had the desert sands buried the temple again?

She pushed past the others and got to the cockpit, holding up the laptop so the pilot could see.

"Can you take us here?"

"It's not far off our route. Why?"

"What's going on, Jana?" Jacob asked.

Jana gave them a recap of what she had learned, ending with the statement, "Look at how big this staff is, and it's only about a third uncovered! I'm thinking there's more uranium-235 hidden inside, and that lead attachment on top was some sort of primitive collimator. But the thing was obviously leaking if the archaeologist died of cancer only a few years after uncovering it."

"I bet that Egyptian professor you mentioned followed the same research trail as you did, and realized he had a bigger storehouse of U-235 he could lay his hands on. But why not go for that instead of grabbing a smaller amount from the Louvre and attracting all that attention?"

"Remember what the Louvre director said. They didn't steal the Staff of Ra, but only an inscription. I'm thinking the staff they stole from the Louvre had some sort of inscription on it that told them something they needed to know. That's why the terrorists took the chance of stealing that first."

"What the hell are you people babbling about?" Florin asked.

"I'll get you up to speed," Jacob said. "Jana, you show Pavel where to touch down."

"I got the coordinates," the pilot said, punching them onto the cockpit display. "We got three problems, though. One, the town is right next to these ruins here that I'm assuming is the ancient fort. Kind of looks like one from above. Problem two is that I'm not seeing the temple."

Jana leaned forward and looked at the images, taken by a British spy satellite and far more detailed than Google Earth. She saw a jumble of ruins and heaps of sand that no doubt buried further remains.

"There," she said, pointing. "That's got the dimensions of a temple. And look at the width of the entrance. That's a monumental gate."

"All right. I'll take your word for it. Now that brings us to problem number three. This town doesn't have an airport, and I don't see an airport within a hundred miles."

Silence. Everyone looked at each other. When no one came up with a response, Pavel shrugged and said, "I can always land on the highway in front of town, as long as I don't bump into a truck or a camel, or rip out the landing gear on a pothole. Then I can wait on the highway while you guys explore some giant radioactive statue. Assuming the cops don't shoot me or one of the two factions doesn't blow up the plane, and the locals don't lynch me, I'll be waiting for you when you come

116

back. In other words, you better be damn sure this is where you want to go."

"You sure are a grim guy," Jacob said. "Why all the negativity?"

"I get shot at for a living."

"I get shot at for a living too, and I'm cheerful 24/7."

"What he means is he's annoying," Jana said. "And to answer your question, no, I'm not sure. I'm not sure about the Suez Canal either. But here's something to consider—thanks to us, the Egyptians just locked down the Suez and are boarding every ship that looks the least bit suspicious. And the CIA, MI6, even Mossad are converging on the area. But who's guarding the town of Ibn Balamon?"

"I'm convinced," Pavel said. "What do you think, Mr. Sunshine and Roses?"

Jacob shrugged. "She's been right a bunch of times before. Let's go for it."

Pavel looked at Alexandru and Florin. "What do you think, guys?"

"We didn't even know about this aspect of the mission until two minutes ago," Alexandru said, cradling his hand. "I say we listen to the archaeologist."

"You got it," Pavel said, turning the plane. "You get to see me land on a Sudanese highway. I sure hope to hell there aren't too many potholes, or you're never going to see the inside of that temple. And even if you do, you better pray they haven't made it before us."

# CHAPTER TWENTY

Dr. Moswen Farag was almost ready. He and his team from The Sword of the Righteous hid out in the temple of Ra on the outskirts of the town of Ibn Balamon. The temple walls shielded them from view. Despite the wear and tear of time, and having been partially filled by sand since the excavation in the 1930s, they still stood taller than a man. Only in one spot could they enter without climbing the cracked masonry, through a gap that had once been the monumental portal, its lintel now half-buried in the sand and serving as a threshold.

Nothing else of the temple remained above the level of the sand. This was typical of ancient sites along the Nile. Until as recently as a hundred years ago, the famous Sphinx at Giza was buried up to its neck; so as it used to be with that famous monument, the grandeur of this once-great temple was mostly obscured.

Very obscured. Judging from the goat droppings scattered everywhere, the locals sometimes used this place to corral their herds.

Not today. He had several of his men in police uniforms block off the area for "security purposes". One of Dr. Farag's officers actually was in the Sudanese police, and had stolen the uniforms for the mission. He also used his ID, that of a captain from the city of El Obeid, to cow the local chief of police into staying away.

The rest of the team was concentrated at one end of the temple, furiously digging, brows gleaming in the harsh sun. They had already uncovered the head of Ra, depicted in his aspect of a man with a falcon head, the sun disc crowning him cracked and half gone. The men worked with a will, six of them shoveling and six more hauling away baskets of sand, and they had already gotten down several feet.

They should be getting to the top of the staff soon.

Dr. Farag stood some distance away atop one of the ruined walls, supposedly to keep watch but also to keep as far from any ambient radiation as possible. He had no desire for martyrdom. He would rather live a long life, see sharia law brought into force the world over, and die a peaceful death secure in the knowledge that he would get his reward in the afterlife.

To ensure this, he had also been taking regular doses of iodine. It helped the body pass radiation through the system rather than letting it build up. A small protection, perhaps, but Allah would grant him the most protection.

He had not told his men the staff leaked, or that the unbeliever who had originally uncovered it had died of cancer within a few years. Nor had he commented on the noticeable number of deformed people and cancer sufferers in the local Christian population. The men and boys who kept their goats here must get daily doses of low-level radiation. Not enough to kill them quickly, but once the staff was uncovered from its mantle of sand …

His men yearned for martyrdom, so they could have it and God bless them. As for the Christians, they deserved a slow death, and he was about to give them a quick one.

Because once the staff was uncovered, he needed to test it.

Dr. Farag looked out over the surrounding countryside. Despite it being an excuse, he took his job as watchman seriously. A year ago, The Sword of the Righteous had been stopped at the last moment from blowing up a dirty bomb in the Suez Canal, and he knew the enemies of religion were doing their best to track him down. Extreme caution on his part was the only thing that had kept them from doing so already. It was not a good idea to underestimate one's enemies.

To the east, he saw nothing but desert. In the near distance were undulations in the sand that he knew from his former profession marked ancient buildings buried beneath the surface. This had been a major complex back in the time when Egypt had ruled over Nubia. To the north, he saw the method of keeping that power—a large tower that remained standing a good ten meters tall, but so crumbled and lacking any interior floors they couldn't use it as a watchtower. All around he could see portions of the fort's surrounding wall, in places several courses high, in others completely missing. The locals had quarried the stone for their own uses. No doubt that big church in town was built from pagan stones. How fitting.

He could tell the fort's outer wall would have surrounded the temple he stood in, and that the remains of the gate, just visible to the south within a grove of palm trees, would have been parallel to the portal of the temple. He imagined the Nubians trying to storm this gate, hoping to throw off Egyptian rule, only for the defenders to open the great cedar doors for them. The surprised and delighted Nubians would have charged in and seen the portal to the temple open. The statue of Ra would have stood in its full glory, staff in hand, and then …

… he wasn't entirely surely what would have happened then. But he intended to find out.

He looked to the west, and there beheld the modern town of Ibn Balamon. It looked like most other Sudanese or Egyptian small towns, a series of flat-topped concrete and stone houses with satellite dishes and TV antennas so people who knew no religion could watch their frivolous shows, and here and there a minaret for the few believers in town.

Right at the town center was a sight that made Dr. Farag's lip curl—a large Coptic church with a bell tower standing higher than any of the minarets.

That would be his first target, whether the staff was in working order, or not. He had a back-up plan.

Just then, as if to mock him, the bells began to ring. It must be time for worship.

Good. They'd all be in one place.

A shout from his men made him turn.

"We found it!"

The men waved to him triumphantly from the pit they had dug. Right at the bottom was a mass of crumpled lead, just as that French archaeologist had said there was.

"Good job! Keep digging!"

"Don't you want to examine the head?"

"We need to uncover the entire shaft of the staff."

"All right."

The men got back to work, building up a rhythm. Now that they had found their prize, they worked even faster than before, cutting down a narrow hole around the shaft of the stone staff, quickly uncovering the stone hand that gripped it. The sand was packed enough this far down that the walls of the pit didn't cave in, but the crew placed boards around the side just in case. They didn't want to lose time to any accidents. They didn't know how much time they had.

Dr. Farag examined the stone staff as it was gradually uncovered. He estimated it would measure a good two meters tall and was as thick as his thigh. Wonderful. It didn't matter that the ancient collimator was destroyed. While he wouldn't get to test it on the local Christians, he could always make another. The Sword of the Righteous had engineers

120

who could make such a thing. The important thing now was to get the Staff of Ra, the true Staff of Ra that was placed here, at this border fort.

The one from the Louvre, that lay in its lead case at his feet, was merely a smaller copy to be wielded by the high priest at Karnak.

Dr. Farag licked his lips and looked warily at the emerging piece of statuary. He felt tempted to pull out the Geiger counter from his bag and turn it on, but he didn't want to spook the men. They were digging so fast. Better not to test their religious zeal.

His walkie talkie crackled.

"Doctor, we are in position around town. Over."

Dr. Farag felt a prickle of fear. Did he hear a bit more static than he should?

Giving the staff a nervous look, he hit the press to talk key. "Good. Do you have the explosives ready? Over."

"Yes, sir. Over."

"Don't put them in place yet. We need to get what we came for, first. Only set them up when I radio you. Stay on watch. Over."

"Yes, sir. Over."

He put the walkie talkie away. He didn't need to fear the local police or anyone else overhearing what they had just said. These were encrypted walkie talkies stolen from the Jordanian police, who used different frequencies than the Sudanese police. No one within a thousand miles could decode what was said over them.

Dr. Farag paced. They were almost there. He eyed the town warily. So many people, and so close. He preferred to work in the shadows, not right next to a population center that might get curious as to what they were doing. His cordon of "police officers" had reported having to push back more than one group of curiosity seekers walking toward the ruins.

The bells at the church stopped ringing. All would be called to prayer there now. First, a sermon. Then the assembled mass of Coptic Christians would pray, sing their hymns, and then take Communion just like the Catholics in Europe. They'd be packed in that church for at least an hour and a half. Plenty of time.

Dr. Farag chuckled. They'd give them a small sample of the severe chastisement they'd give the world.

"We're getting there, doctor!" the crew leader said, sounding out of breath. Sweat poured down their faces now and the diggers panted like dogs in heat. He hoped none of them would pass out.

"Good. Keep digging!"

They went after it with renewed gusto. Dr. Farag took out his phone and examined the inscription on the staff from Karnak, then double-checked the translation he had put in his notes. Yes, they had a way forward. They had a way to disrupt the world so much that it would launch global jihad.

A sparkle of light in the sky made him look. Just an airplane in the distance. He'd seen many pass along this route, although this one looked smaller and flying lower than most.

Another crackle on his walkie talkie distracted him.

"All clear on the road coming into town, doctor. Over."

"Good. Maintain vigilance. Over."

"Doctor!" one of the diggers gasped more than shouted. "We've uncovered the whole thing."

Dr. Farag turned and looked. There it was, completely uncovered. The sun god's stone hand grasped a stone shaft engraved with hieroglyphs, the base of the staff resting on the partially uncovered plinth of the statue. The French had gotten only about a third of the way down before their field season had ended all those years ago, so he and the diggers were the first to see the entire Staff of Ra in more than three thousand years. He felt a thrill of discovery, an awe at the wonders of the past like he used to.

He quickly tamped that blasphemous feeling down.

*Forgive me, Allah. A moment of weakness. What I really feel is a thrill that Your will can now be done.*

He hopped down from his perch and went over to a large duffel bag he had set nearby. A couple of sweating, panting diggers joined him. The rest backed away to take position on various points of the temple wall and gate.

Dr. Farag felt a tingle of unease as the two diggers joined him. One idiot still carried his shovel. His *metal* shovel. The former Egyptologist unzipped the duffel bag and pulled out a Tyvek radiation suit. He hurried to get it on. His companions grabbed the other two Tyvek suits in the bag and donned them.

Now fully protected, Dr. Farag walked over to the statue, sweat already trickling down his back. It was stifling in this thing. Sudan was so hot. Even for an Egyptian it was hot. He dreamed of taking jihad to nicer places like England or Alaska. Someplace cool.

His two companions huffed and puffed as they followed him. This was why he didn't have the dig crew wear these suits while uncovering the Staff of Ra. They'd have died of heat prostration even quicker than they'd die of radiation poisoning, and he had no time for fainting jihadists on this mission.

Dr. Farag hopped into the pit and studied the vertical line of hieroglyphs carved deeply into the stone staff.

"It's well preserved," he said with audible relief. "Go fetch the case."

The men ran off and returned carrying a long lead tube, struggling under the weight.

Dr. Farag pressed two symbols on the ancient text—one of the sun disc and the other of a whip.

There was a loud click, and the front side of the statue's staff fell off.

Dr. Farag grabbed it, surprised at its lightness. It was delicately carved of the thinnest stone.

And inside the hollow statue's staff rested a lead tube running almost the entire length of the stone staff. Dr. Farag grabbed the tube and pulled it out with the help of his two younger and much stronger assistants.

Once out, they could see the lead tube was open at the top, the U-235 exposed to the ruined collimator.

"It would have been a great weapon once," Dr. Farag said, "and it will be so again. Let's get it into the case."

The lead case he had fashioned was slightly too large for it. No matter. He had erred on the big side since he didn't know the exact dimensions of this ancient wonder weapon.

Snapping the case shut, they hauled it out of the pit. Then his assistants helped him out.

One of his assistants unzipped his Tyvek suit and shucked out of it, taking a deep, grateful breath.

"Thank God we're safe from the radiation and can breathe properly again. I was melting in there."

*You are safe now, my friend, but you were not safe before. No matter. You'll get your reward in paradise.*

Dr. Farag began to get out of his suit too.

Just as he finished, there was a shout from the wall, facing town. At the same time he heard the crackle of his radio, which he had left behind at the spot where he had been standing.

"What is it?" he called over. "What's going on?"

123

The reply was drowned out by an approaching jet engine. Beyond the pointing sentinels on the old temple wall, beyond the little town with its church spire, a private jet was coming in for a landing.

"Where is it touching down?" he shouted, struggling out of his suit, and running over.

The answer got drowned out by the jet engine.

As he climbed onto the wall, he saw for himself.

The jet was landing on the highway just outside of town, less than a kilometer from his position. His heart turned to ice.

*They've found us.*

He grabbed his walkie talkie.

"Set the charge! Wire the church doors shut! Set the timer for ten minutes. We can lure the infidels to the church. When they try to defuse the bomb, the booby trap will blow them up too!"

"Yes, doctor. We're getting into position now."

Before the radio cut off, he could hear gunfire and the screams of civilians in the background.

Dr. Moswen Farag smiled. The unbelievers had arrived too late. He already had what he came for. The Sword of the Righteous would be victorious, and they would send hundreds of infidels to hell.

# CHAPTER TWENTY ONE

Jacob gritted his teeth as the private jet owned by the SAS bumped and shuddered down the poorly paved Sudanese highway. In the cockpit, Pavel gripped the yoke, desperately trying to keep the plane from veering off the pavement as he let out a string of curses in Polish. While Jacob didn't speak Polish, he discovered that many swear words in the language were similar to Russian, which he did speak. This was turning out to be an education.

Peering out the window, he saw the town of Ibn Balamon, a small, dusty cluster of flat-roofed houses with a few minarets and a large church dominating the skyline. Beyond, he saw a ruined heap of stone that Jana said was once an Egyptian fort.

Closer to the plane, he saw several civilians running away from the road, panicked at their sudden arrival. Another loud curse from Pavel heralded the appearance of a car that veered off the road and trundled to a stop in the sand.

"We're going to have a hell of a time convincing the local authorities we're the good guys," Jacob said.

"I never thought I'd say this," Florin said, "but I hope The Sword of the Righteous has launched an attack. It's the only way the local cops won't use us for target practice."

The jet shuddered to the final stop. The fort looked only about a kilometer away, on the other side of town just past the church, which satellite imagery had shown stood in the main square. Pavel hit the button for the door to open and the gangway to lower.

"Let me do the talking," Jacob said. "We'll play like we're mercenaries. Since there's a large Christian community here, they won't be any friends of The Sword of the Righteous."

Everyone piled out. To his surprise, Alexandru came too, his wounded hand in a sling, the other hand gripping a pistol. He gave the Romanian a nod of respect.

The immediate area was abandoned. Their dramatic appearance had scared everybody off. As they ran into town, they found everything locked up tight. No one was on the streets, the shutters of the shops were down, and all windows firmly shut.

Once they got away from the roaring of the jet engine, they began to hear the crackle of gunfire coming from the direction of the main square.

From the direction of the church.

"We have to go check it out," Jacob told his companions. "Florin, you're with me. Jana, Alexandru, head for the temple."

"Splitting up?" Florin said. "Tactically that's a crap idea."

"We don't have time for tactics. And if you and I light some hellfire against the terrorists near that church, maybe it will distract them from whatever's happening at the temple."

"Let's go," Jana told Alexandru.

They ran off, Jana gripping her assault rifle, the wounded Alexandru with his pistol. Jacob gave them a worried glance then ran for the town square, Florin at his side.

Jacob had no idea if he had made the right decision, but the gunfire proved that at least some of the terrorists were at the church. Maybe all. He wasn't sure if any were at the temple. He had to go after the enemy he could find.

The gunfire sounded closer. Yes, it was definitely clustered around the church.

They passed a family running in the other direction. When they spotted two heavily armed foreigners, they screamed, held up their hands, and moved to the other side of the street.

"What's going on?" Jacob demanded.

They kept running.

Next they came across an old man hobbling down the street with the assistance of a cane, looking fearfully behind him.

Jacob stopped him. "What's going on?"

The man looked him up and down, obviously surprised at Jacob's fluent Arabic.

"Are you a Christian?" he asked.

"Yes."

*If you are willing to accept a really, really loose definition of Christianity. I was baptized, anyway.*

"Some men dressed as police came to town this morning. They've wired the church doors shut during services, and have placed a bomb on it! It's only by a miracle that I wasn't in there myself."

"And the firing?"

"Our police, who are mostly Muslim, God bless them. They are fighting the terrorists but they are losing."

126

"Thanks."

Before they could move on, the old man grabbed Jacob's arm.

"I will show you an alley that will get you to the church square unseen."

They retraced their steps half a block and turned down a narrow space between two buildings. The firing continued. Jacob tried to contain his impatience at their guide's slow steps.

They got behind the building and the old man stopped, pointing around the corner. Jacob took a peek.

While the local man had indeed brought them to an alley that opened onto the church square, he hadn't exactly made a good tactical assessment. The alley ran straight as an arrow behind three long buildings before ending at the square, which looked about as wide as a football field. A portion of the church standing on the opposite side of the square was visible.

But between their position and the square were a pair of police officers, kneeling right at the opening of the alley and using the corners of the buildings as cover while they fired at an unseen opponent.

Jacob ducked back.

"There are two police officers there. Can you tell if they're yours?"

The old man took a peek, squinting for a moment before coming back around the corner.

"My eyes aren't what they used to be. All I see are two figures in uniform. I'll walk down there and see."

"They might shoot you!"

The old man nodded. "Then you will know what side they are on."

"But … "

Before Jacob could finish his objection, the old man hobbled around the corner and out of reach. Jacob looked around the corner, unsure whether to chase him or not, and found him already several steps along the alley. With one hand he gripped his cane. With the other he held aloft a wooden cross he had pulled from his pocket.

Jacob pulled back out of sight, cursing.

"Officers!" he heard the old man shout. "I wish you God's blessing in saving the church!"

The crack of a gunshot. A cry. The thud of a body hitting the earth.

Jacob snarled and jumped around the corner. The old man lay in the dust, mouth agape, bleeding out his last, and one of the cops was just turning back toward the square. He did a doubletake when he spotted Jacob.

127

That was the last thing he saw. Jacob's bullet took him in the head, and his second shot went right through the body of the other fake police officer.

Jacob and Florin sprinted down the alley, stopping for only a moment to check the old man was, indeed, dead.

"We'll save your church for you," Florin whispered.

"Damn right we will," Jacob said through gritted teeth.

Jacob checked the two terrorists were down for the count, then gave a quick peek out of the alley.

What he saw was utter confusion. A couple of cops lay dead in the open square—whether real or fake, he couldn't tell—and men in police uniforms fired at each other from half a dozen hiding places around the square. Some used a corner of the church for shelter. Others were inside a large shop. A couple more hunkered behind the engine block of a parked car. Three more fired from the upper story of a private residence.

All wore identical uniforms. Jacob supposed this was a small enough town that the local cops knew who was who, but he had no idea, and no way to find out.

*Well, maybe there's one way. A really stupid way.*

He peeked again to check on the church. The doors were lashed shut with baling wire and a large bomb was attached to it. There was an electronic fuse and a timer, but he couldn't see how much time was left from this far away.

"Crap. That thing is going to blow at any minute."

Florin took a peek.

"It's a shaped charge. See how the casing is like a bowl with the wide end stuck on the door? I bet it's going to blast shrapnel right through the crowd, and it's big enough to kill a whole bunch of them."

"Yeah. And with a whole crowd packed in for services, it's going to do maximum damage."

Florin pointed. "Maybe we can work our way around to the left and get to that wide road over there, then hotwire a car or truck to drive up to the front and use as cover."

"Good idea, but there's no time. Cover me."

"Cover you? What are you going to do?"

"Something really, really stupid. You ready?"

Florin gave him a doubtful look. "Yeah. Are you?"

"No."

Jacob bolted into the square, in full view of both warring factions. He shouted at the top of his lungs, "I'm going to disarm the bomb! I'm going to disarm the bomb!"

That told him and Florin which cops were the terrorists.

The men behind the car and the men in the shop opened up on him.

Jacob dove and rolled as bullets hit the dirt all around him. He heard Florin get into the game, firing at the men who had now revealed themselves for what they were.

He sprang to his feet and lay down suppressing fire on the guys behind the car, his bullets clanging harmlessly off the engine block. The two behind it kept their heads down. Glancing at the shop, he saw a shadowy figure in one of the windows flail and fall, taken out by the SAS man who still had his back, or maybe by one of the real policemen.

The gunfire slackened as the terrorists had to focus on the men firing at them rather than the crazy foreigner exposing himself in the middle of the battlefield.

He made it to the church door and saw three things that made him want to turn back around and run away as fast as he could.

First, the shaped charge looked bigger than it had from the other side of the square, and the old, thin wood of the door would be no barrier. The bomb was sure to kill most of the parishioners locked inside.

Second, the wiring was too complex for a simple bomb. He got the impression there was a booby trap here somewhere, something that would blow him up if he tried to defuse it.

Third, the timer was down to two minutes.

***

Jana and Alexandru ran down a side street, trying to give the battle in the town square a wide berth.

A cop appeared at the end of the street, stopped as if surprised, and leveled his AK-47. They ducked down another street before he got a chance to fire. The last thing they needed was to get fired at by the local police force. They hadn't seen any terrorists yet. Perhaps they were all at the church?

Jana didn't count on it. Some were probably still at the temple, trying to uncover the Staff of Ra. Or maybe they had gotten it already and had decided on one last terror attack before going on their way.

At least the streets were abandoned. A civil war had wreaked havoc in this country for more than a year now. When people heard gunfire, they locked themselves in their homes or shops and didn't dare look out.

Jana spotted the old walls of the fort to her left and saw they had veered off course. They got to another intersection, took a quick look around, and headed left.

The fort loomed up ahead. There were a couple of blocks more of the town before the buildings petered out into desert. She could just make out some of the lower walls of the surrounding ruins.

They came to another intersection. When they peeked around the corner, bullets made them spring back.

It was the police officer again, and he had found a comrade.

They were half a block away in a doorway, both armed with AK-47s.

"You speak Arabic," Alexandru said. "Shout to them that we're on their side."

"There's no guarantee they'll believe me and we don't have time to convince them." She pulled out a smoke grenade. "I'll throw this into the street and we'll run across."

"All right. Let's fire above their heads as we do. That might keep them down and keep them from spraying the area."

"Good idea."

The road was narrow enough that even firing blind, the two officers would have a chance of hitting them.

Jana tossed the smoke grenade into the middle of the street. It detonated with a bang and started emitting thick, black smoke. Jana put her assault rifle on full auto and ran across the gap, firing high enough to leave the two Sudanese cops safe. Alexandru added fire with his pistol.

No return fire came. Within two seconds, they were safely across.

"Let's get there before they can catch up with us," Jana said.

They sprinted to the outskirts of town without any more trouble, then cut right, away from the fort, to a jumble of ruined masonry that gave them cover from the temple. They didn't see any sign of life.

Jana wasn't fooled. Something told her there were terrorists still in the temple, hidden out of sight.

"The entrance is around the right side, opposite from the fort," Jana whispered. "Let's work our way around and see if we can take a peek inside."

"All right," Alexandru said.

Jana crawled behind the masonry until she got to a series of low dunes that probably hid more archaeological features. She followed these for a time, then looked over the top to see where she was.

She discovered Alexandru was lagging behind. Because of his wounded hand, he couldn't crawl on his hands and knees like her, and was instead squat-walking like a crab. It looked uncomfortable as hell and he was sweating profusely, but he didn't complain.

Jana could see they were almost in line with the temple entrance. She moved a bit more to the right and peeked again, now able to look directly through the entrance. She didn't see anyone inside.

But she saw a recently excavated pit, with a heap of sand piled on either side.

In the middle, she could just make out the top of something in stone.

The statue?

A flicker of movement to her right caught her eye. A couple of figures humped over the wall and were gone.

They had moved too quickly and were too obscured for her to make them out.

"Did you see that?" Alexandru said.

"Yeah."

"They went over the wall on the opposite side from the city. I'm thinking they got that staff thing and are making a getaway."

"That's exactly what I'm thinking," Jana said. "Let's go."

They ran low behind the sand hillocks, came to a clear spot, and darted over to the cover of some more crumbling masonry. Peeking between a gap in the stones, Jana spotted an older, somewhat heavyset man carrying a duffel bag and a lead tube a couple of meters long, about the size of the missing Louvre artifact, next to three men in police uniforms carrying a much larger lead tube, struggling under its weight.

They were only about thirty yards away, moving into the desert.

"Oh my God, the terrorists are dressed as cops," she whispered.

"Then those guys we passed in town—"

Alexandru never got to finish his sentence. A shot rang out behind them. The SAS man arched his back, gasped, and fell.

131

# CHAPTER TWENTY TWO

Jacob stared at the complex network of wires spreading out from the bomb like some sinister spider's web. He saw wires that obviously connected to the timer, some more that obviously led nowhere, and some others he wasn't sure of.

There were so many!

That was the point. They'd heaped wires upon wires so that no one would be able to figure out which went were, which would set off the booby trap, and which would defuse the bomb.

Especially when the timer read one minute and thirty seconds.

A shot thumped into the church door. Another cracked off the stone doorframe. Jacob pulled out both of his smoke grenades and tossed them to either side. A smokescreen rose, obscuring him from view.

That only helped a bit because the terrorists still knew where he was.

A bullet hit the ground at his feet, making him jump. Another hit the door, snipping a wire and making him yelp.

It wasn't one of the booby trap wires. And it didn't stop the timer either.

One minute and twenty seconds.

The gun battle behind him continued. He heard the thud of a grenade. Jacob squatted down to make less of a target, a bullet whizzing through the air just where his head had been a second before, and tried to focus on the wires.

The terrorists had been tricky. The wires came in red, green, and black, but he could tell they weren't color coordinated. Superficially they appeared to be, but he isolated two dummy wires that were of two different colors.

He pulled out his Bowie knife and cut those two wires to get them out of the way and leave fewer distractions.

His Bowie knife sprang out of his hands, hit the door, and bounced back to hit him in the head handle first.

"Ow! Speaking of distractions!"

He picked up his Bowie knife and found the tip had been shot off. It was now embedded in the wood just an inch from the timer.

132

At least the edge of the knife could still cut if he could only figure out which wires to actually sever.

One minute.

He peered at the timer. It was clamped to the shaped charge, the wires mostly hidden from view because they went directly into it. But several more went around the edge of the door and inside the building.

Those, or at least some of those, led to the booby trap, another shaped charge ready to blast outwards and kill him if he snipped the wrong wire.

It would probably set off this shaped charge as well, sending a blast inwards to kill the congregation, which he could hear wailing, shouting, and praying inside.

So the two shaped charges would be at different heights. They wouldn't be right opposite one another or the blasts would cancel each other out. There would be shrapnel, sure, but not nearly as much than if the terrorists placed one higher than the other.

Should he shout inside? Ask someone there to help him?

Fifty seconds.

Too time consuming. He'd have to calm down a civilian and have him or her walk him through what they saw on the other side of the door. He'd never get it done before the blast hit.

So which wires really led to the timer and which were false leads? And which would set off the booby trap if he cut them? Because there were sure to be trick wires among this mess.

A three-round burst thudded into the upper part of the door in a neat arc.

That had come from nearly behind him. The terrorists had shifted position, which meant they were no longer pinned behind cover.

Which meant they were winning.

Another thud of a grenade.

Forty seconds.

Jacob traced a couple of wires that disappeared behind the seam of the door just level with the shaped charge. They must be false, unless they had kinked the wire, of course.

He had to take that chance. He cut them with his broken Bowie knife.

OK. That left four wires. One must be to disarm it, one must be to set it off, and the two others could either be false leads or also connected to the booby trap.

And he had no idea which was which, and no real way to guess.

133

Thirty seconds.

Wiping his brow, he shifted his attention to the shaped charge on his side of the door. He spotted one obvious false lead and cut it, stripping it away.

That left far too many.

He isolated one that he was pretty sure was a false lead and moved to cut it.

His blade poised just a millimeter above the wire. Something else had caught his eye.

The wires were so enmeshed with each other that he hadn't noticed something before. They weren't just layered over one another to cause confusion, they were layered over one another to hide the fact that a couple of them were spliced together.

Cleverly spliced, too. The outer part of the insulator had been left in place. Only the backside of the insulation had been shaved away with a razor, as well as a tiny bit of the insulation of the wire beneath, leaving the exposed copper of the two wires touching. Not a proper splice where you tie two wires together, but enough of a contact to run a current through.

Suddenly he saw this network of wires in a whole different light.

Ten seconds.

He pressed his cheek against the door and studied the network of wires. They crisscrossed worse than the Los Angeles highway system, but he could make out which intersections were spliced and which weren't. There was a splice there ... and there ... and (oh!) there.

Jacob stepped back and looked at the network of wires one last time.

He raised his Bowie knife, hesitated, then slashed one of the wires.

The timer stopped.

Three seconds.

"Wow! A whole three seconds? Last time I got down to one second."

A burst of fire behind him. Jacob ducked and spun around. The smoke from his grenades was clearing and he saw two shadowy figures beyond the screen running for him. One pirouetted and fell. The other burst through the smoke, an AK-47 raised high.

"Die, infidel!"

Jacob slashed at the man's arm, making him lose his grip on the assault rifle, then grabbed him and slammed him into the door, which rattled on its hinges. He got a grip on the hair on the back of the terrorist's head and slammed his face into the door, again and again until the man went limp and sank unmoving to the ground.

The final smoke cleared, and he saw Florin and a couple of local policemen come out into the square. Florin gave him a thumb's up.

"That was the last of them!" he shouted.

Jacob grinned and began unraveling the baling wire that held the church doors shut.

***

Jana gasped as Alexandru fell over, a gunshot having pierced his body. She rolled, popped up into a kneeling position, and fired.

The two fake policemen were behind another sand hillock about twenty yards behind her.

Her first shots missed, but they were close enough for the terrorists to put their heads down and allow Jana to scramble to a less exposed position.

Then firing came from both directions, from the two false policemen and the three men who had dropped the large lead tube with a thud.

Jana hit the dirt. She was caught in the crossfire between two enemy forces.

"When that happens," her father used to say, "you need to even the odds as quick as you can."

Lying prone, she pulled the pin from one of her fragmentation grenades and, still holding the safety lever so the fuse wouldn't start, edged a bit more to one side.

The firing had stopped. She was fully out of sight. But she needed to act now before those guys shifted position to prepare for their next move.

She leapt up, saw the two guys behind her still in the same position, and chucked the grenade just as bullets came at her from two directions.

By some miracle she dropped back down to Earth with her body intact.

The grenade went off. Grabbing her assault rifle again, she crawled toward the guys she'd just thrown the grenade at. The men with the tube had gone silent, no doubt because they were getting into better cover than the exposed flatland she'd caught them on.

First, she'd make sure her rear was secure and those two guys were really dead, and then she'd circle around and hunt down the professor and three fighters with the lead tubes.

She also needed to reconnoiter a bit and make sure there wasn't anyone else lurking around here. She couldn't take the chance of getting it wrong and getting hurt or killed. If they got away, it would be the end of everything.

The distant crackle of gunfire and the thud of a grenade in town told her Jacob and Florin had gotten into some action.

She couldn't worry about them now. She had found the main object of the mission right here, and she was all alone.

Crawling between the sandy humps, the occasional potsherd or chunk of masonry hinting at what might lie beneath, she made it to the two false policemen who had tailed them out of town.

One was obviously dead. The other lay by his side, gasping, his face turned away from her. The sand around them was soaked with blood.

Jana withdrew before the wounded man spotted her. She couldn't run the chance of making noise while putting him out of his misery, and he was in no condition to get up and follow her anyway.

Now for the main event.

She made a wide circle around the area where she had spotted the archaeologist and his followers, keeping behind ruins and heaps of sand as much as she could, crawling quickly across the more open areas, eyes and ears perked for any sign they were close.

When Jana was almost parallel with the spot where she had first seen them, a soft sound to her left made her pause. She couldn't see anything in that direction because she was right up next to a heap of stony sand immediately to her left.

Another soft sound to her right, and seemingly further away. In that direction were a series of foundations of mudbrick, the outbuildings of the fort and temple complex.

Again the soft sound to her left. It sounded close, as if right on the opposite side of the heap of sand.

The crunch of a boot crushing an ancient potsherd underfoot confirmed it.

She pulled out her last fragmentation grenade and heaved it up and over the little hillock.

As it exploded, the detonation punctuated with a scream, she rushed to her right, straight toward the other enemy.

Just as she thought, a head poked up about ten yards away from behind a crumbling foundation of mudbrick.

She raised her gun to fire, and a shot from her right took her by surprise. The third terrorist had gotten behind her!

The bullet plucked at her clothing but didn't carve flesh.

She dropped down in the middle of the ground that was far too exposed. For the moment she was out of sight. She crawled forward, hoping she'd make it to cover in time.

The guy behind the mudbrick wall showed himself first. Rising up, he aimed at her.

Jana got off the first round. The terrorist flailed and fell.

A shot behind her made her turn.

The third terrorist stood not ten yards from her, gripping an AK-47. He stared at her, frozen for a moment, then fell dead.

Alexandru stood behind him, pistol in hand. He swayed from side to side, made a feeble gesture toward the desert, then his eyes turned up in his head and he fell.

Jana rose and looked where Alexandru had indicated.

The professor was huffing it across the desert about a hundred yards away, the smaller lead tube tucked under his arm, a duffel bag flapping on his back.

Jana ran after him, vaulting over the foundations of ancient walls and weaving between sand dunes. After a minute she passed the large lead tube, tucked behind the base of an altar or plinth as the terrorists had turned to confront her.

*Thank God it's too heavy for the professor to run off with.*

He was having trouble with the smaller one too. She gained on him, and he was huffing and puffing and struggling so much under his burden that he didn't even notice.

*Maybe I can take him prisoner. I'd love to be present at the questioning of this scumbag.*

When Jana got within ten yards of her quarry, he finally heard her and turned around.

He gaped, tripped over a fragment of statuary, and fell. Jana laughed.

"Stay where you are," she ordered.

The professor stared at the gun leveled at him.

"Dr. Moswen Farag, former Egyptologist, you're under arrest."

He snorted. "You think you have authority over me, you unbelieving bitch?"

"This gun has authority over you. You might not know me, but I'm an archaeologist too. How did you go from someone who loved his nation's history to someone who'd blow it up? Even the most callous, ignorant member of the public wouldn't do that."

Dr. Farag smiled. "Yes, I was lost once, and then Allah opened my eyes. To think I once studied pagan things. It makes me shudder. At least now I am pure. And I've been shown a way for my past sin to bring future glory. I'll help bring shariah law to the world. All remnants of the pagan past will be swept away, and arrogant Western sluts like you will be put in their place."

He sat up. Jana gestured with the gun.

"My place is right where I am, and your place is in prison. Or the grave if you don't freeze this instant."

He didn't. Instead, he leapt up, discarding both the lead tube and the duffel bag, and continued to run.

"Stop!"

Jana bore down on him. He didn't have any obvious weapons, and so she decided to bring him in.

Still he ran. This guy just didn't know when to quit.

She body checked him like a hockey player, and felt a good deal of satisfaction when he did a faceplant into the ground.

He came up quicker than she anticipated, snarling, reaching out for her.

Jana kicked him in the nuts. He let out an "oooof" and fell right back down.

"That one's for the pyramids!"

The roar of an engine. A four-by-four came out of nowhere, driving right for her. An Egyptian man in civilian clothing leaned out the window, firing at her with an AK-47.

Jana cursed and dove for cover, bullets chasing her until she got behind a couple of blocks of masonry sticking out of the sand.

The four-by-four screeched to a stop in a plume of sand. Jana rose and fired, taking out the first man to emerge.

But there were three more, and they laid down a fire that forced Jana to duck for cover.

And there was nowhere to go. The two stone blocks she had gotten behind stood isolated.

*If they come at me in a pincer movement, I'm dead. Damn it, why did I use up all my grenades!*

She kept glancing to the left and right, waiting for the inevitable as more bullets cracked off the stone.

*One's going to maintain a suppressing fire while the other two come around either side.*

The firing stopped. A door slammed, and she heard the four-by-four driving away.

"Damn it!"

She rose up and started firing, taking out the back window of the four-by-four, causing it to swerve. She thought she saw a spray of blood inside, and then it went over a hillock and out of sight.

Jana sprinted after it. By the time she got to the hillock, the vehicle was a good two hundred yards away. Jana emptied her magazine at it, thought she saw one or two sparks off the body of the vehicle, then ejected the magazine, slapped in another, and fired until the four-by-four was out of range, a dwindling dot disappearing into the vastness of the Sudanese desert.

Cursing, she retraced her path. The lead tube, which no doubt contained the Staff of Ra from Karnak that the terrorists had stolen from the Louvre, was gone, as was Dr. Farag's duffel bag.

Jana grimaced. She had failed. She had stopped them from taking the main supply of U-235, but she had still failed. The Sword of the Righteous may not have enough uranium to make a nuke, but they could still make a dirty bomb. She wondered if they'd reconstruct the ancient collimator and recreate the weapon of the ancient Egyptians. That might be even worse.

A gleam of sunlight off something on the ground made her look.

A cell phone. Dr. Farag's cell phone? It was around the spot where she had gotten into that scuffle. It must have fallen out of his pocket and in their rush to get away, the terrorists hadn't noticed it.

She picked it up and started jogging back to the town of Ibn Balamon.

# CHAPTER TWENTY THREE

*A field just outside Edinburgh, Scotland*
*That same day*

Aaron Peters sat inside the cool stone chamber, the rough stone walls that hemmed him in illuminated by the soft glow of his remote control touchscreen.

He sat inside a dolmen, a stone chamber built in the Neolithic period to house some chief or prominent warrior. He liked the irony of hiding inside an archeological monument. It made him think of Jana. He hoped he could see her soon, and that somehow they'd reconcile.

He also liked that this ancient monument to a warrior was housing a modern warrior who was also defending this country.

Because Scotland was in peril, and no one but himself and a handful of others knew it.

The drone he controlled hovered out of sight above the low clouds over downtown Edinburgh. It didn't matter, because the infrared imagery on the drone he'd bought in Denmark could look right through the cloud cover.

He was gazing down on Princes Street, the wide thoroughfare running from the famous castle through the historic town. Crowds of tourists and locals appeared as red blobs walking along the cooler background of the rainy Scottish street. The time in the upper righthand corner of the screen indicated that the limo should leave the underground parking garage any moment now.

Callum Fraser was known for his punctuality. He always ate lunch at his exclusive club (founded in 1762) on Wednesdays if he was in Edinburgh, and always left within a few minutes of 2:00 p.m. to head to his office outside the hustle and bustle of the city.

He always avoided the main highway and took a smaller country lane that would providentially keep him away from any excess casualties.

Sitting cross-legged on the damp earth, Aaron spared another glance at the small grave chamber around him, placing a hand on the cool stone. He hoped he wouldn't be disturbed. This dolmen sat in a farmer's field within easy range of the city and had the advantage of allowing him to remain out of sight. The only problem was that hikers sometimes came to look at it. He himself had posed as a hiker coming here. He hoped the steady drizzle would keep them away, but you never knew with the Scots. They thought nothing of hiking in anything less than a hailstorm.

A limo emerged from the underground car park and turned downhill on Princes Street. Aaron Peters increased magnification.

While he couldn't see the license plate without descending through the cloud cover and almost surely being spotted, the vehicle was the same make and model as the one Callum Fraser used. It was a special reinforced model that cost millions and was generally reserved for heads of state.

Fraser wasn't a head of state, but he came pretty close. He was Scotland's richest man, with deep investments in North Sea oil and natural gas, as well as a diverse portfolio in other business interests. He had recently purchased a controlling interest in Scotland's most popular supermarket chain. What he could do with that made Aaron tremble.

Because Fraser Callum wasn't just a multimillionaire and one of the globe's Fortune 500. He was a major funder of The Order.

And as such, he needed to die.

Not only would that disrupt The Order's funding, but it would help bring to light anyone else high up in Fraser's business empire linked with the shadowy group. Too much money was funneled through shell companies for Fraser to do it alone, and a careful study of the changes in behavior among the various vice presidents and chief accountants after his death would hopefully reveal who else was in on it.

Aaron Peters waited patiently as the limo moved down Princes Street, then took a left to head into the Edinburgh suburbs on its way to Fraser's privately owned office building on the edges of town.

He had no scruples about killing this unarmed civilian on his way to work.

To the world, Callum Fraser was just another rich man, someone who weathered the occasional protest for his role in the fossil fuel industry but who otherwise was respected in the corporate world for his business acumen and in the arts world for his generous patronage.

To Aaron Peters, he was one of the biggest civilian funders of terrorism on the planet.

Which in his book, made Fraser no longer a civilian.

He followed the limo on screen, keeping above the vehicle as it drove out of town. The traffic was still too heavy here for him to make the strike. He didn't want civilian casualties. He reduced the magnification to check the surrounding area, especially the road ahead. Yes, once the limo got past this last housing development there were no pedestrians and almost no traffic. Just another couple of minutes now.

Faint voices made him curse under his breath. He set down the screen and crawled to the small entrance of the dolmen, barely big enough for his wide shoulders to squeeze through.

Keeping his head well within the interior shadows, he looked out.

On the far side of the field walked two women and a man, each with a day pack and rain gear, expensive hiking boots on their feet.

Aaron Peters cursed again. They were heading this way. One even stopped and took a photo.

Perfect. Just perfect.

He scrambled over to the control screen for the drone. The limo was stopped at a red light.

"Come on, come on," he muttered.

The light must have changed because the limo moved forward.

The voices grew louder, drawing nearer. He hoped they couldn't see the thin aerial he had set up on the backside of the dolmen, picking up signals from his control screen through a crack in the stone slabs to transmit it into the sky to the drone a couple of miles away.

The limo was just getting past the last housing development. Aaron checked the surrounding area, saw that there were no pedestrians or vehicles within the blast zone, and zoomed in.

The voices grew clearer. The man was talking.

"These dolmens are scattered all over the British Isles and Europe. They started on the continent at around 5000 BC and began to be built on the British Isles about a thousand years later. This one apparently was erected around 3500 BC. It was excavated in the eighteenth century by the antiquarian … "

*Shut up already. I'm trying to concentrate.*

He locked on target. With a final look around the surrounding area, he raised his forefinger over the fire button.

" … they found the remains of a bronze sword inside that you can see at the museum in Edinburgh … "

Aaron Peters hit the fire button. Two miles away, a miracle of miniaturized explosives streaked down on the limousine.

Callum Fraser's armored limo was one of the best that money could buy—strong enough to resist an RPG round to the sides, or a medium-sized landmine to the bottom, or even a grenade to the top.

But it couldn't take an armor-piercing military grade missile to the roof.

The screen was filled with the blast. Aaron didn't take the time to watch. Boots squelched in mud just outside. He stuffed the screen into his daypack, zipped it up, and crawled out of the dolmen.

"Oh!" one of the women cried in surprise, cutting off the mansplainer mid history lesson.

"Sorry to startle you," Aaron said with a grin. "Just relaxing out of the rain."

"I just heard thunder," the other woman said, looking toward town.

"Communing with the dead?" the man asked Aaron.

"Yes! I mean, no. Meditating. Very soothing. Have a nice day."

He walked around to the back of the dolmen. One of the women muttered something under her breath. He snatched the little aerial off its perch and stuck it inside his jacket, then strolled across the field to where he had parked his jeep.

*** 

Stage two. Aaron Peters had driven several miles down a country road to a scenic overlook that would have been scenic if not for the fact that the drizzle had turned into a steady downpour, obscuring what must have been a beautiful view of fields of heather cut by a babbling stream. His drone had remained in place over the target, and when Aaron had finally taken another look, he saw that the limo was a flaming wreck. No chance of survivors despite the fire truck and ambulance speeding to the rescue. The emergency crews would be lucky if they could pick apart which bits belonged to Callum Fraser and which belonged to his chauffeur and bodyguard.

Now he had a new target, one that was just around the next bend, hidden by some woods atop the bluff where the scenic overlook was situated.

Just a mile down the road stood a gas station with an "out of business" sign displayed prominently out front. Chains and padlocks hung on the pumps and the lights were off.

The gas station might have been out of business, but a very different business went on in the garage just behind. Aaron maneuvered the drone above the cloud cover to directly above the garage and began to lower it.

He moved a little to the right, so that it would come to rest right on the back edge of the flat roof, just above a window and out of sight from the road.

Easy now. Easy. Can't make any noise when it comes down. While the drone was engineered to run as silently as possible, the rotors still made noise and the whole drone was pretty heavy. He couldn't come banging down on the tar paper roof. Hopefully what noise he did make would be drowned out by the drumming rain.

Slowly, ever so slowly, he brought the drone lower, praying that it wasn't spotted. Everyone was inside, but if someone came along just now, the second half of his mission would be ruined.

The drone came to rest on top of the garage. He panned the camera and didn't see anyone. Then he hit another control, and an extendible arm lowered from the chassis to place a metal cup down on the roof. Inside the cup was a highly sensitive microphone that could listen through walls. He switched it on.

Male Voice One: " … so once that's done, we can make a move."

Male Voice Two: "Brilliant. It's about time."

Female Voice Three: "Will he be able to get through? They're in a state of emergency."

Male Voice Two: "They set it all up ahead of time. They're a good outfit."

Female Voice Three: "A crazy outfit."

Male Voice One: "Useful idiots."

There followed a couple of minutes of footsteps, tapping on a keyboard, and a tea kettle whistling. Then came some unimportant conversation about tea and biscuits. Aaron waited with the patience born of long experience until they got back to the good stuff.

Male Voice One: "Angus is right. They run a tight ship."

Female Voice: "They screwed up once already."

Male Voice Two: "That screw-up still caused a ton of disruption. If they get the Staff of Ra, they'll be the most useful tool we've ever drawn in."

Female Voice: "I hope you're right."

The sound of a spoon clinking as someone stirred milk or sugar into their tea. Nothing more for five minutes.

Aaron decided he'd waited long enough. He needed to hit them before they heard their boss's limo had just gone up in a fireball and they decided to make a run for it. He couldn't wait around forever for them to say something useful.

He headed out, driving for the closed service station that was now a hideout for Callum Fraser's assistants in The Order. He left the sound on.

As he got within sight of the gas station, appearing to anyone inside as just another vehicle driving along this back country road, he hit the controls to make the drone shoot up and angle downwards to fire its final bunker-busting miniature missile.

Female Voice: "I hope they got the Staff of Ra."

Male Voice One: "What's that sound? Is that a drone?"

*Damn it!*

Aaron hit the fire button. Up ahead, the drone hovering a couple of hundred feet above the service station fired its high-powered death. An instant later, every window and door in the place blew out. The detonation was so strong it cracked Aaron's windshield and shook his jeep enough that he almost veered off the road.

He regained control of his vehicle and screeched to a stop just outside the ravaged building.

Hopping out, he grabbed his compact Heckler & Koch MP5 submachine gun and sprinted through the smoking front doorway.

Inside, the garage had been converted into a machine shop with a row of ruined and burning computers on one side. The computers were ruined, and the remains of what looked like a half-completed minisub stood on a platform. Interesting.

He couldn't see much else except the body of a man lying face down near the minisub. Loud coughing to his left made him go in that direction.

The smoke was so thick he almost tripped over the next dead man, and then coming out of a side room staggered a woman, bloodied from head to toe.

"Freeze!" Aaron shouted, aiming his MP5 at her. "We can make a deal!"

Her eyes focused and she bit down on something in her mouth. A moment later she went into convulsions and collapsed.

Just like the rest of them. They always bit down on a cyanide capsule to evade capture. Without fail. He'd never even seen an Islamist organization that had so much devotion among its rank and file.

Aaron did a quick search of the building, grabbing a thumb drive and the hard drives of all three computers. They looked past recovery, but you never knew. The techies back at the CIA lab could work wonders.

He sprinted out to his jeep and sped away before anyone else came along.

As he drove, he punched controls to the drone to have it rise above the cloud cover and follow.

Once he had made it a few miles and made a few turns, he felt like he could relax. He'd made a clean getaway. The most important cell in the United Kingdom had been taken care of.

And it had left him with a question.

What the hell was the Staff of Ra?

He knew someone he could ask, the very same person he most wanted to see.

Aaron Peters smiled. It looked like the family reunion would come sooner than expected.

# CHAPTER TWENTY FOUR

*Jacob Snow's residence to the east of Athens, Greece*
*One week later*

Jana Peters read the email from her colleague with a growing sense of amazement.

And a deep sense of despair.

After the CIA had decrypted Dr. Moswen Farag's phone, they had sent her the photos on it. They showed the Staff of Ra that had been stolen from the Louvre, complete with a hieroglyphic inscription down the gold shaft.

Of the doctor, there was no trace. By the time Jana had reunited with Jacob, the professor and his followers were long gone. Every available spy technology was brought to bear to scour the desert, the Sudan, and the entire region, but it was like the sands had swallowed him up. He had planned his escape well.

But they'd hear from him again. She was sure of it. And this email was proof.

An Egyptologist at the Louvre, briefed by the French government and ordered to remain silent to the press and public, had translated the inscription.

*Hail the Sun God!*

*The withering power of Ra defeats all enemies.*

*At the great temple in Nubia, the signs of Ra and the whip are the keys to power.*

*At the hidden temple the signs of Ra and life are the keys to power.*

*Both are of equal power, and the priest of Karnak has the key in his staff.*

"Jacob, could you come in here?" Jana called over her shoulder from where she sat on Jacob's sofa in his modern-style living room, with its floor-to-ceiling windows overlooking the Aegean. The fact that those windows were bulletproof and the entire house built like a fortress didn't detract from the scene's beauty.

Jacob padded into the living room in a bathrobe, his hair still damp from the shower they had taken together a few minutes before.

"Want to go for a swim?" he asked. When he saw her expression, his face fell. "Uh-oh."

"Uh-oh indeed, take a look at this translation of the Staff of Ra from Karnak."

He read over her shoulder.

"Um, I'm going to need a little help here."

"This line, 'At the great temple in Nubia, the signs of Ra and the whip are the keys to power' is about how to open the casing of that statue the terrorists uncovered in the Sudan. There was a catch on the hieroglyphics for the sun disc and the whip. Pressing those made the casing come off."

"And at this hidden temple you have to press the 'signs of Ra and life,' so the sun disc and the ankh?"

"Very good. How did you know about the ankh?"

"I dated a yoga instructor who wore one."

"If you start making jokes about yoga positions, I'll slap you."

"I'm merely citing my sources like a good academic. So do you have any idea where this hidden temple could be?"

"Zero. What most concerns me is this last line, 'Both are of equal power, and the priest of Karnak has the key in his staff.'"

Jacob grimaced. "Yeah, this means that the statue at the hidden temple has as much U-235 as the one in the Sudan. The techies said it was ultra-pure, and weighed in at more than 60 kilos, enough to make a nuke. But what's this key in the staff? The Sword of the Righteous still has that staff."

Jana slumped. "I don't know what the key is. If I hadn't screwed up, we could examine the staff and find out."

Jacob put an arm around her. "It's not your fault. You had to go after them alone."

"You would have beat them," Jana murmured.

Jacob gave her a squeeze. "I have way more training than you, and we wouldn't have even had the chance if you hadn't figured out the link to the temple at Ibn Balamon. There aren't any records at the Louvre?"

"No. After it was discovered that the staff was radioactive, it was put away in that secret storage level and never examined again. The archaeologist who discovered it made an exterior examination, so the key must be something internal."

"So these bastards get to try again."

Jana nodded. After a moment, she asked, "Do you think they already know where this hidden temple is?"

"Who knows? We have an international manhunt out for them, and thanks to that phone you recovered we've taken out three cells of their organization in Tunis, Bamako, and Beirut. We've also tracked down some individual operatives. They're on the ropes but not down for the count. I think Dr. Farag and his friends are going to have to lay low for a while."

"Which gives us some time, hopefully." Jana let out a sigh. "I'm afraid we're going to have to skip that swim. I need to do some research."

"Into what?"

"The location of a temple that was a state secret more than three thousand years ago. I haven't the faintest idea how the hell I'm going to find it."

***

Dr. Moswen Farag rubbed his shoulder and grunted at the lingering pain. That unbeliever bitch had shot him clear through the muscle as they drove away. If it hadn't been for some quick first aid, he would have bled to death.

At least they had made it out, first to an isolated cove on the Red Sea coast, where some brothers in The Sword of the Righteous had picked them up in a fishing boat and sailed them to Yemen, where the cell in Sanaa had put them up in a farmhouse a few kilometers outside of town.

He hadn't set foot outside ever since. He was too afraid of drones.

Dr. Farag yawned and took another sip of rich Yemeni coffee to revive himself. He wasn't sleeping well at all—the pain, the worries about drones, and every step of a sentry outside made him think a gang of Navy SEALs was about to burst in and do to him what they had done to Bin Laden.

And all because of that damn phone. It had fallen from his pocket during the fight in Sudan. They must have recovered it. That was the only explanation for how the unbelievers had been able to martyr so many brothers.

Still, he had the Karnak staff, and he knew the secrets of what lay within.

And he had a pretty good idea of where the hidden temple was.

He just needed to do a bit more research. An operative in Cairo was making his way down here with some old books and a thumb drive of data that would, God willing, tell him all he needed to know.

The way was perilous, however. The Egyptians had locked the country down.

Luckily, The Sword of the Righteous had planned ahead. Egypt was too important to their operations to lose, so before the Giza operation, the cells in that country had meticulously devised safehouses and transport routes that would elude the eye of even the best detectives and spies the government had.

It would all take time, first for the operative to make it here, and then for him to do his research.

Then he would have to set up an entire operation wherever this hidden temple to Ra turned out to be.

And during that time, the enemies of religion would be hunting him.

He rubbed his shoulder again. Perhaps he should stay on the move, find another safehouse once the operative got here. Yes, he would start setting it up now. He didn't want to get droned like so many of those impulsive idiots in ISIS had, and he didn't want to get his head blown off by a Navy Seal like Bin Laden.

He needed to use all his wits to elude capture. The stakes were too high to lose now.

Because if he managed to find the hidden temple, and if the other Staff of Ra remained intact, The Sword of the Righteous would become a nuclear power.

Meanwhile, the engineering division was working on a pair of collimators, both for the staff he had and the staff he would find, God willing.

The assassination division was hard at work too.

Their task was to find that heretic bitch who had shot him. Not to kill her, but to bring her to him.

Dr. Moswen Farag smiled despite the ache in his shoulder. If the assassination division succeeded, that would be a good day, a very good day.

For him, not for her.

# NOW AVAILABLE!

## TARGET SEVEN
### (The Spy Game—Book #7)

"Thriller writing at its best... A gripping story that's hard to put down."
--Midwest Book Review, Diane Donovan (re *Any Means Necessary*)

**From #1 bestselling and USA Today bestselling author Jack Mars, author of the critically acclaimed *Luke Stone* and *Agent Zero* series (with over 5,000 five-star reviews), comes an explosive new action-packed espionage series that takes readers on a wild ride across Europe, America, and the world—perfect for fans of Dan Brown, Daniel Silva and Jack Carr.**

The hunt for a legendary lost artifact has Jacob in a wild chase across the Mediterranean, in a race against time to catch the nefarious organization after it. But in a shocking twist, when Jacob realizes who the artifact is destined for, the stakes could not be higher—or more dangerous.

An unputdownable action thriller with heart-pounding suspense and unforeseen twists, TARGET SEVEN is the seventh novel in an exhilarating new series by a #1 bestselling author that will make you fall in love with a brand-new action hero—and keep you turning pages late into the night.

Future books in the series will soon be available.

"One of the best thrillers I have read this year. The plot is intelligent and will keep you hooked from the beginning. The author did a superb job creating a set of characters who are fully developed and very much enjoyable. I can hardly wait for the sequel."
--Books and Movie Reviews, Roberto Mattos (re Any Means Necessary)

## Jack Mars

Jack Mars is the USA Today bestselling author of the LUKE STONE thriller series, which includes seven books. He is also the author of the new FORGING OF LUKE STONE prequel series, comprising six books; of the AGENT ZERO spy thriller series, comprising twelve books; of the TROY STARK thriller series, comprising five books; and of the SPY GAME thriller series, comprising seven books.

Jack loves to hear from you, so please feel free to visit www.Jackmarsauthor.com to join the email list, receive a free book, receive free giveaways, connect on Facebook and Twitter, and stay in touch!

## BOOKS BY JACK MARS

### THE SPY GAME
TARGET ONE (Book #1)
TARGET TWO (Book #2)
TARGET THREE (Book #3)
TARGET FOUR (Book #4)
TARGET FIVE (Book #5)
TARGET SIX (Book #6)
TARGET SEVEN (Book #7)

### TROY STARK THRILLER SERIES
ROGUE FORCE (Book #1)
ROGUE COMMAND (Book #2)
ROGUE TARGET (Book #3)
ROGUE MISSION (Book #4)
ROGUE SHOT (Book #5)

### LUKE STONE THRILLER SERIES
ANY MEANS NECESSARY (Book #1)
OATH OF OFFICE (Book #2)
SITUATION ROOM (Book #3)
OPPOSE ANY FOE (Book #4)
PRESIDENT ELECT (Book #5)
OUR SACRED HONOR (Book #6)
HOUSE DIVIDED (Book #7)

### FORGING OF LUKE STONE PREQUEL SERIES
PRIMARY TARGET (Book #1)
PRIMARY COMMAND (Book #2)
PRIMARY THREAT (Book #3)
PRIMARY GLORY (Book #4)
PRIMARY VALOR (Book #5)
PRIMARY DUTY (Book #6)

### AN AGENT ZERO SPY THRILLER SERIES
AGENT ZERO (Book #1)
TARGET ZERO (Book #2)

HUNTING ZERO (Book #3)
TRAPPING ZERO (Book #4)
FILE ZERO (Book #5)
RECALL ZERO (Book #6)
ASSASSIN ZERO (Book #7)
DECOY ZERO (Book #8)
CHASING ZERO (Book #9)
VENGEANCE ZERO (Book #10)
ZERO ZERO (Book #11)
ABSOLUTE ZERO (Book #12)

Made in the USA
Monee, IL
21 December 2023

50282453R00094